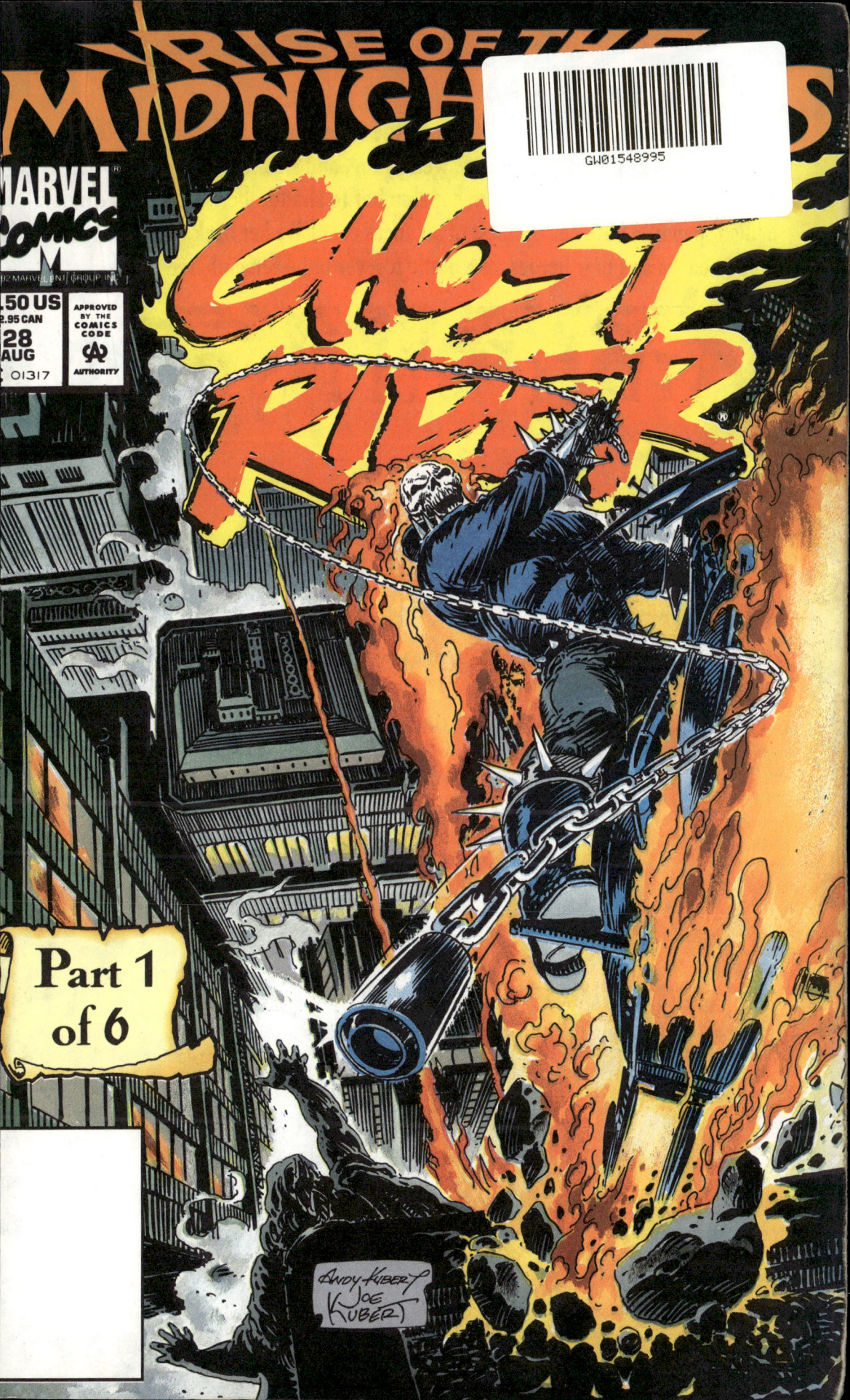

For eons, the walls between our earth and the supernatural realms have held fast ... until now. Now those walls are weakening, and LILITH, Queen of Evil, Mother of Demons, has risen from her slumber to shatter the walls and free her hellish spawn. Only the strangest of alliances can drive her back ... a union of old enemies and new heroes, in a battle forever to be remembered as the ...

GHOST RIDER #28
PART 1

Writer: HOWARD MACKIE
Penciler: ANDY KUBERT
Inker: JOE KUBERT
Colorist: GREG WRIGHT
Letterer: JANICE CHIANG
Editor: BOBBIE CHASE
Editor In Chief: TOM DeFALCO

SPIRITS OF VENGEANCE #1   Part 2
MORBIUS #1   Part 3
DARKHOLD #1   Part 4
NIGHTSTALKERS #1   Part 5
GHOST RIDER #31   Part 6

WHEN INNOCENT BLOOD IS SPILLED, A SPIRIT OF VENGEANCE IS BORN, AND DANNY KETCH FINDS HIMSELF TRANSFORMED. STAN LEE PRESENTS...

BROOKLYN, NEW YORK...

KRAK

GHOST RIDER

MURDERERS, YOU CANNOT ESCAPE MY--

--VENGEANCE!

RISE OF THE MIDNIGHT SONS PART 1

VISIONS

For eons, the walls between our earth and the supernatural realms have held fast ... until now. Now those walls are weakening, and LILITH, Queen of Evil, Mother of Demons, has risen from her slumber to shatter the walls and free her hellish spawn. Only the strangest of alliances can drive her back ... a union of old enemies and new heroes, in a battle forever to be remembered as the ...

SPIRITS OF VENGEANCE #1
PART 2

Writer: HOWARD MACKIE
Artist: ADAM KUBERT
Colorist: GREGORY WRIGHT
Letterer: MICHAEL HEISLER
Editor: BOBBIE CHASE
Editor In Chief: TOM DeFALCO

GHOST RIDER #28   Part 1
MORBIUS #1   Part 3
DARKHOLD #1   Part 4
NIGHTSTALKERS #1   Part 5
GHOST RIDER #31   Part 6

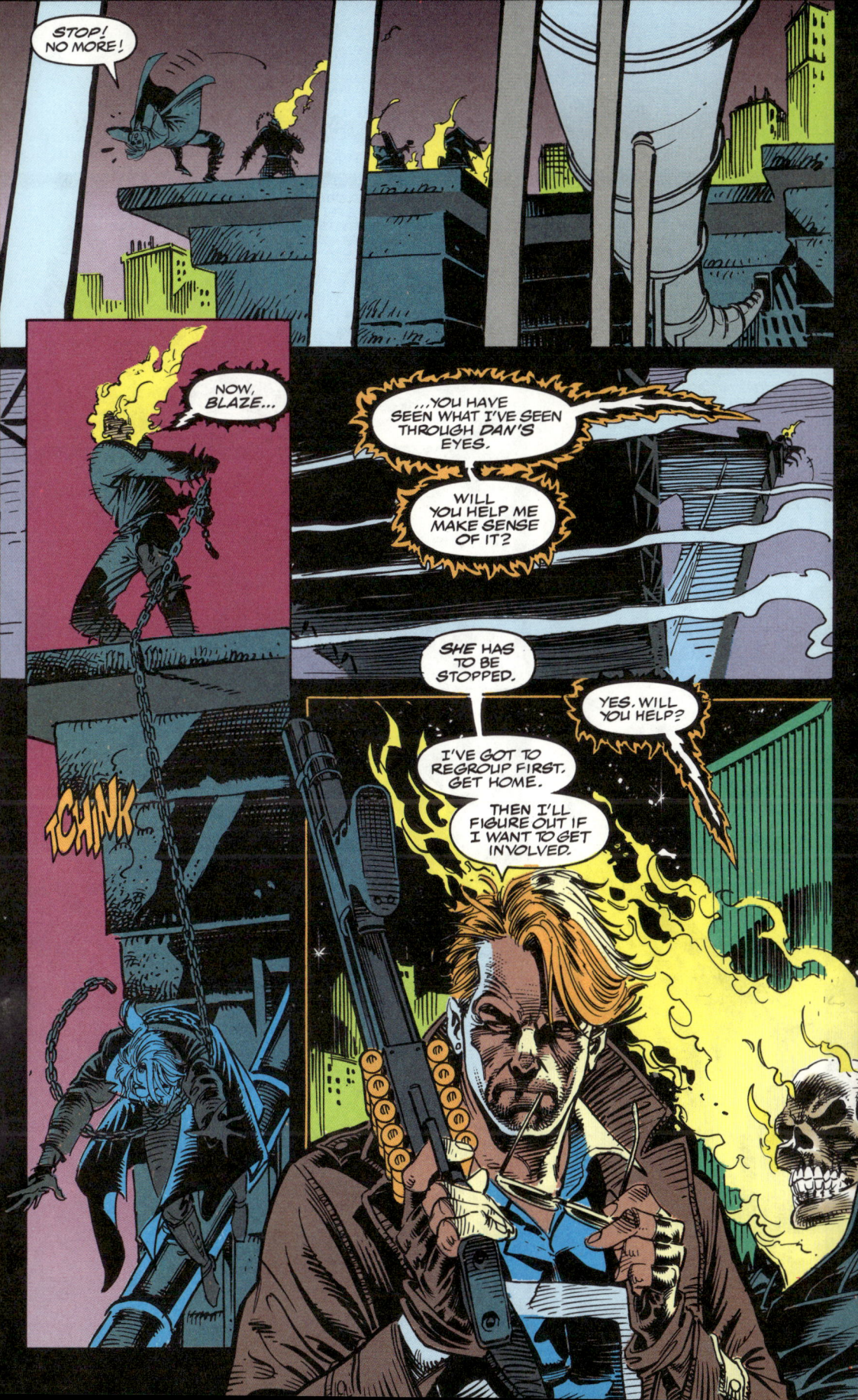

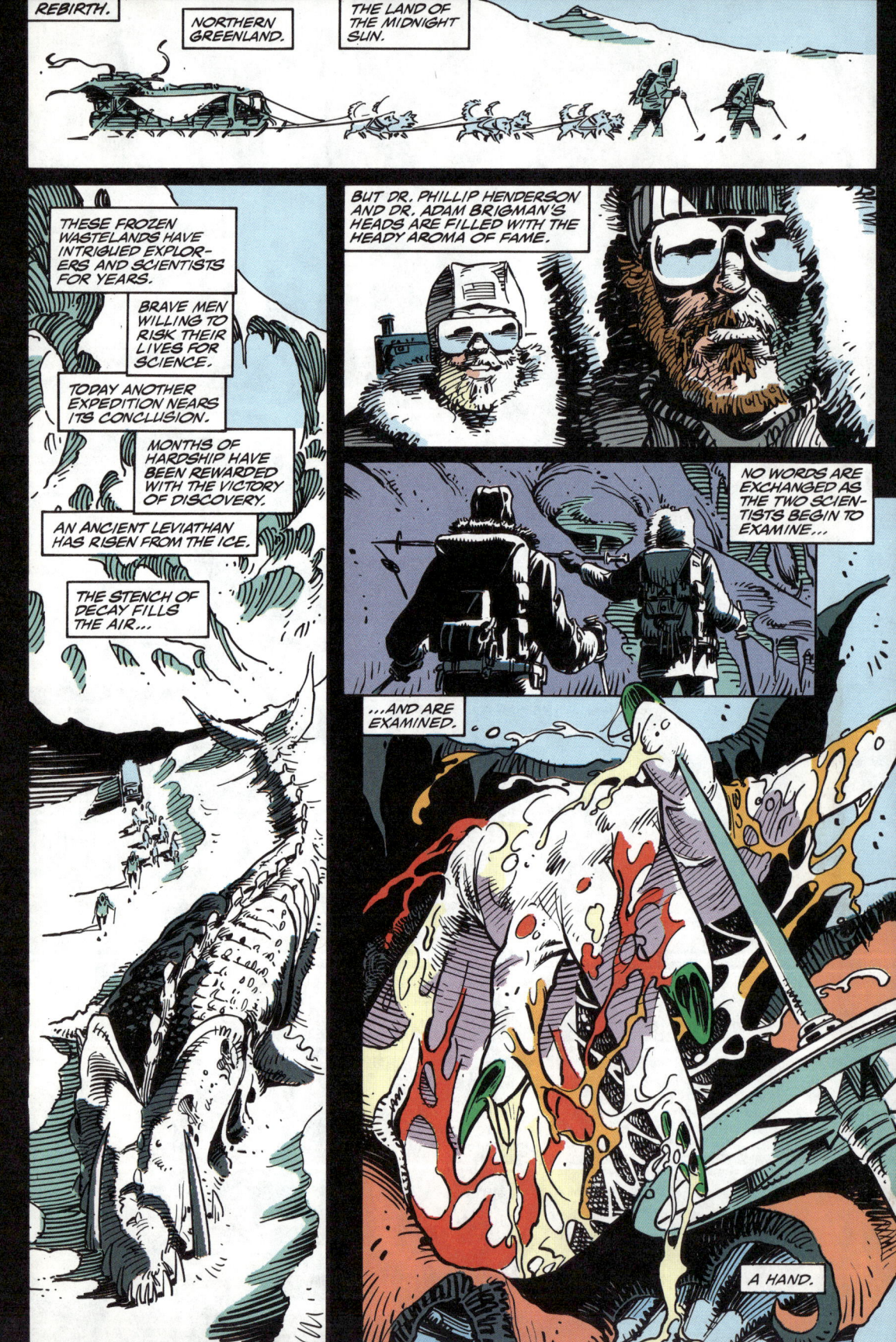

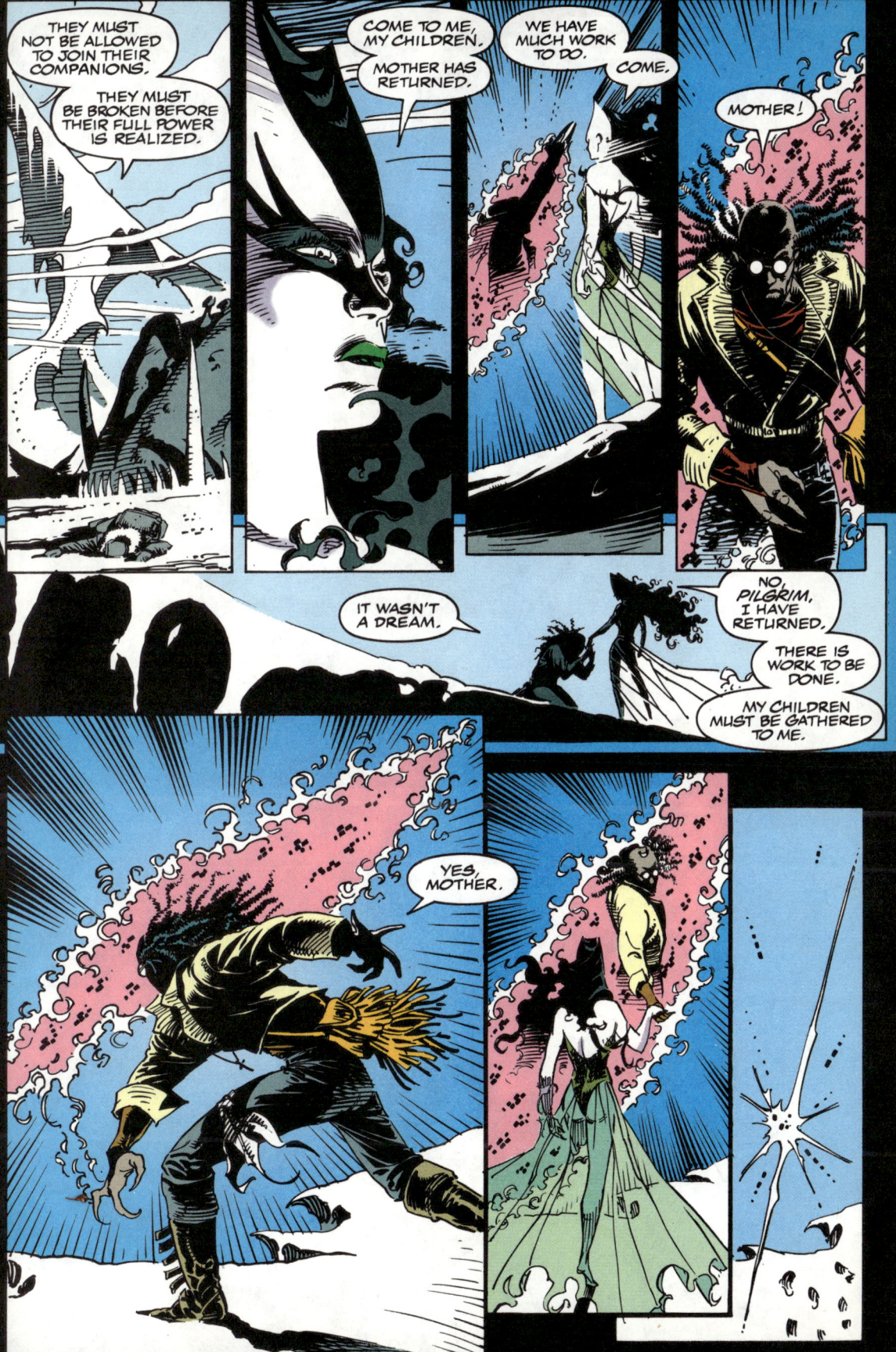

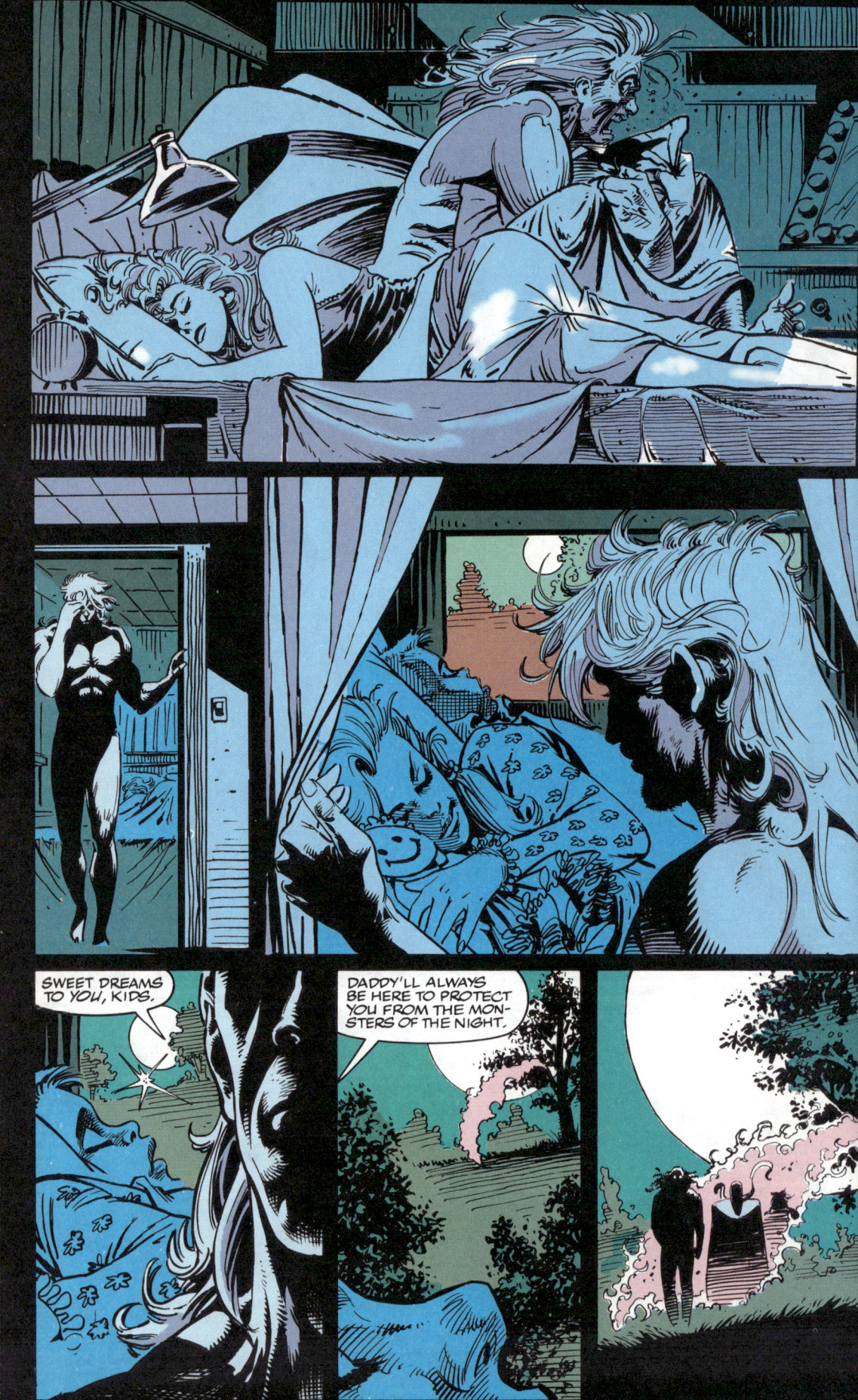

"HOW WILL THEY FIND US?"

"BLAZE WILL FIND US, I SENSE THAT THERE IS MORE TO HIM THAN EVEN HE IS AWARE."

"IT BEGINS. LET US BE QUICK ABOUT IT."

"-:ACK:- CREED....?"

"FREE THE BOY."

"BLACKOUT, DO NOT HARM THE BOY. I'LL TALK TO THE FATHER, HE'LL SEE HE HAS NO CHOICE."

"MY MOTHER IS LILITH. YOU MAY HAVE HEARD OF HER BY NOW. YOU, GHOST RIDER, AND OTHERS POSE A THREAT TO HER. ONE OF YOU MUST DIE. SHE HAS COMMANDED. I DON'T WANT TO HARM YOU OR YOUR SON."

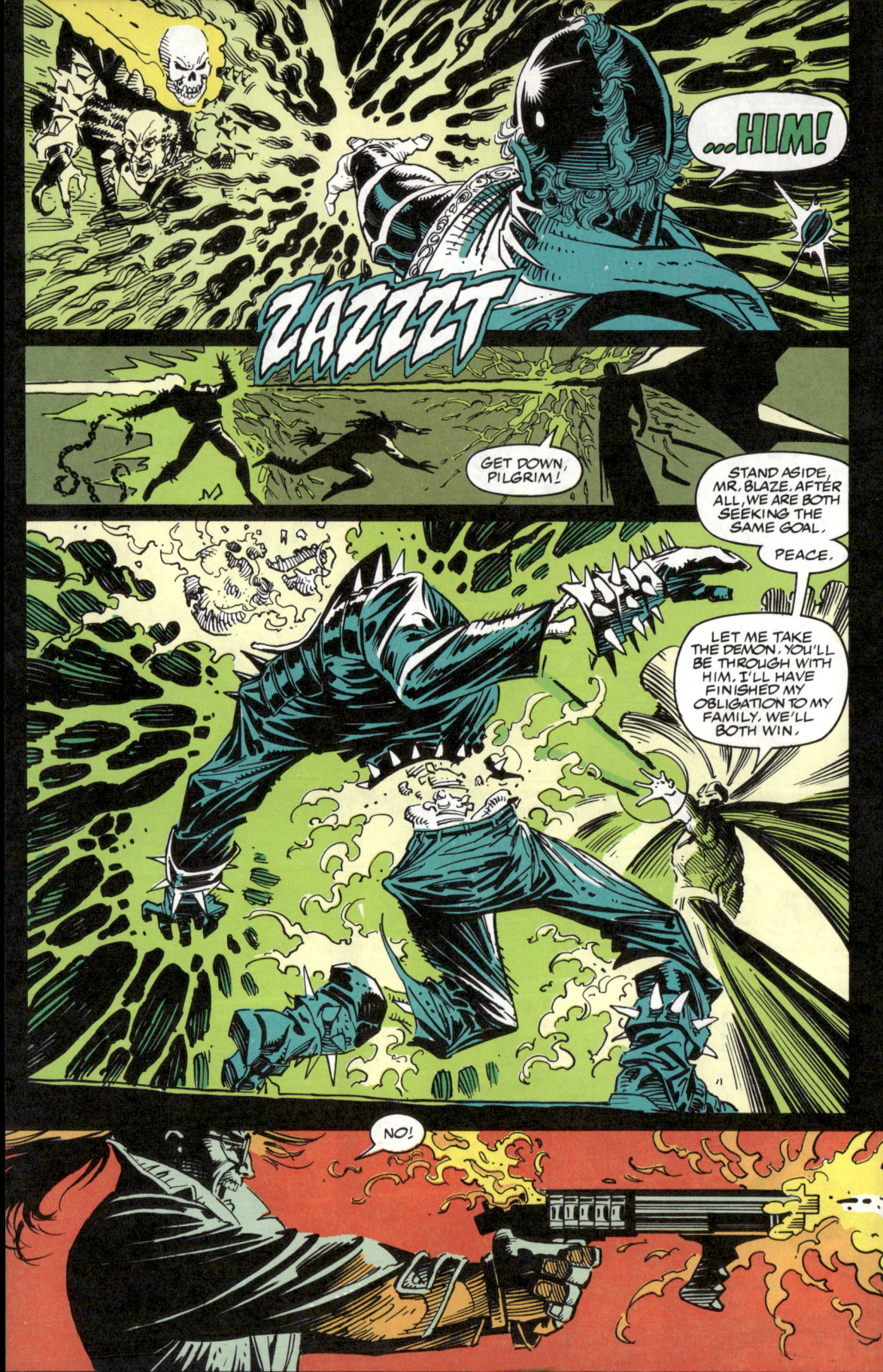

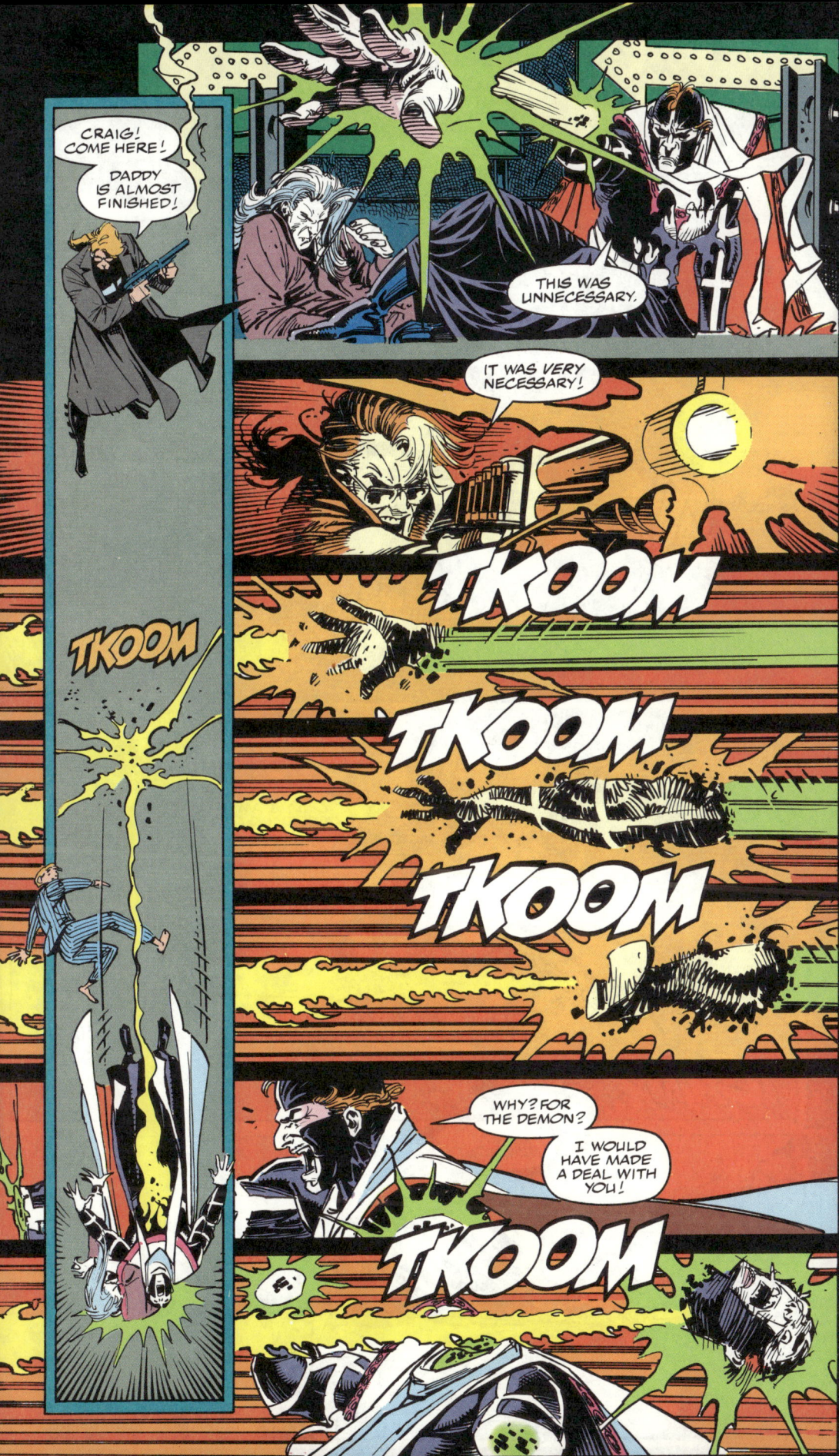

For eons, the walls between our earth and the supernatural realms have held fast ... until now. Now those walls are weakening, and LILITH, Queen of Evil, Mother of Demons, has risen from her slumber to shatter the walls and free her hellish spawn. Only the strangest of alliances can drive her back ... a union of old enemies and new heroes, in a battle forever to be remembered as the ...

MORBIUS #1
PART 3

Writer: LEN KAMINSKI
Penciler: RON WAGNER
Inker: MIKE WITHERBY
Colorist: GREGORY WRIGHT
Letterer: JANICE CHIANG
Editor: BOBBIE CHASE
Editor In Chief: TOM DeFALCO

GHOST RIDER #28   Part 1
SPIRITS OF VENGEANCE #1   Part 2
DARKHOLD #1   Part 4
NIGHTSTALKERS #1   Part 5
GHOST RIDER #31   Part 6

THERE.

BELOW.

THE REDHEAD.

HE CAN SMELL HER.

STENCH OF CHEAP PERFUME.

RANCID SCENT OF CLOTHES THAT SHOULD HAVE BEEN WASHED RATHER THAN WORN.

BUT BENEATH THAT...

OHHHHHH...

THE SWEETNESS.

"NOW!"

HIS ACHING THROAT SCREAMS, "NOW!"

THE ENDLESS EMPTINESS IN HIS STOMACH SHRIEKS "YES! YES!"

HHAA?

Mgbn...

"HE BECAME *DESPERATE* AS HIS TIME RAN OUT.

"HE STARTED *EXPERIMENTING* WITH STRANGE, *UNTESTED* TREATMENTS.

"SERUMS EXTRACTED FROM VAMPIRE BATS.

"*ELECTRO-SHOCK* THERAPY.

"IT *WORKED*... SORT OF.

"OH, HE'D STAVED OFF THE DISEASE, ALL RIGHT-- BUT THERE WAS A HORRIBLE *SIDE EFFECT*.

"THE TREATMENTS HAD *TRANSFORMED* HIM INTO A CREATURE WHICH HAD TO FEED ON *HUMAN BLOOD* TO LIVE.

"A... *LIVING VAMPIRE*.

"AFTER HE ALMOST KILLED *ME*,* HE *AVOIDED* ME COMPLETELY, RATHER THAN RISK IT HAPPENING *AGAIN*.

"LATER, HE WENT INTO A KIND OF *REMISSION*, AND GOT A CHANCE TO *REBUILD* HIS LIFE.

* *FEAR #31.*

"I PRAYED HE WOULD *SUCCEED*, THAT MAYBE WE COULD BE *TOGETHER*. AGAIN.

"MOST RECENTLY, HE SUPPOSEDLY FOUGHT *SPIDER-MAN*.*

"BUT THEN I HEARD THAT HE'D *RELAPSED*, AND HAD ENCOUNTERED THE OCCULT EXPERT *STEPHEN STRANGE*.

* *DR. STRANGE #10.*

* *SPIDER-MAN #13.*

"WHEN I HEARD, I *KNEW* WHAT I HAD TO *DO*.

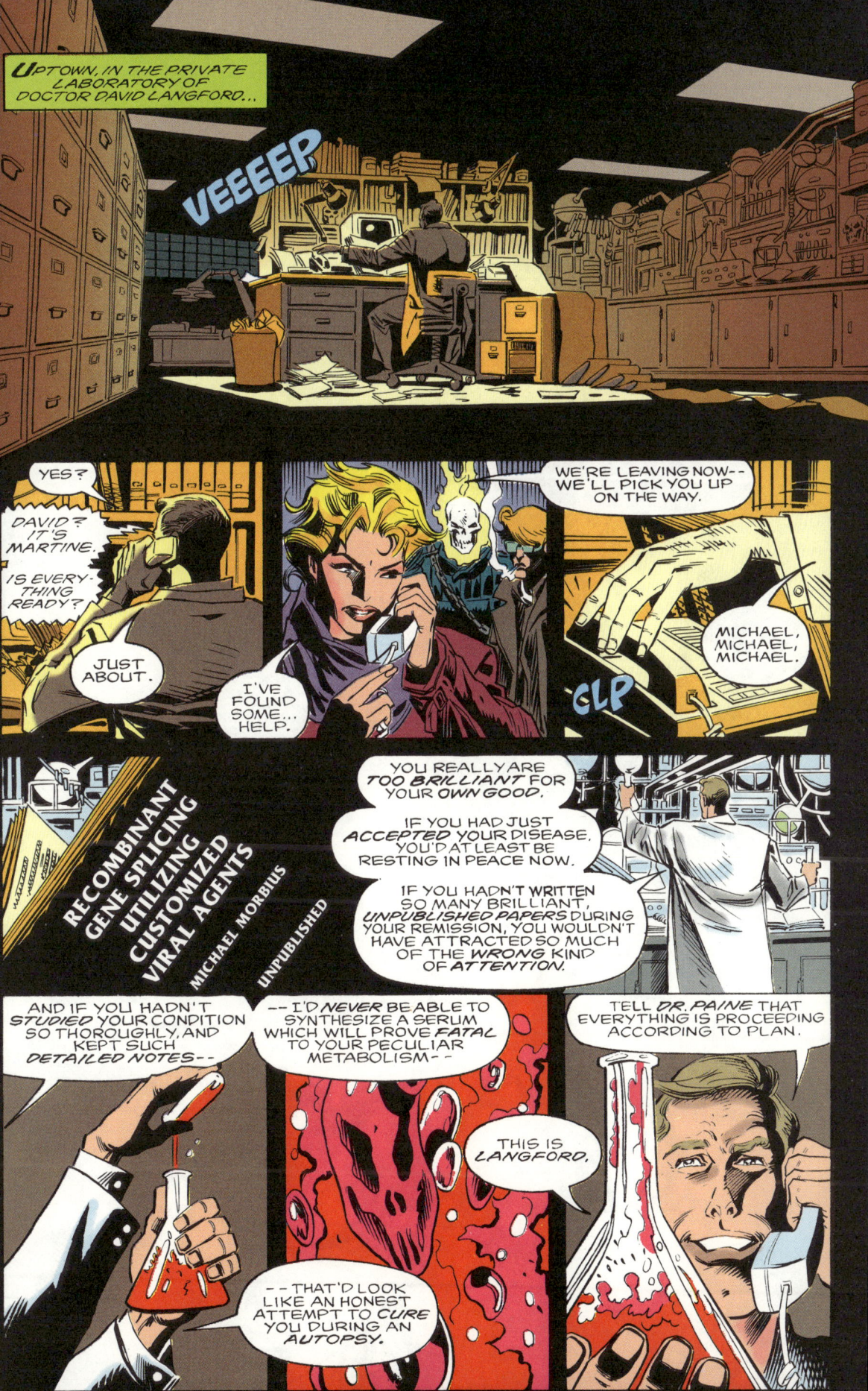

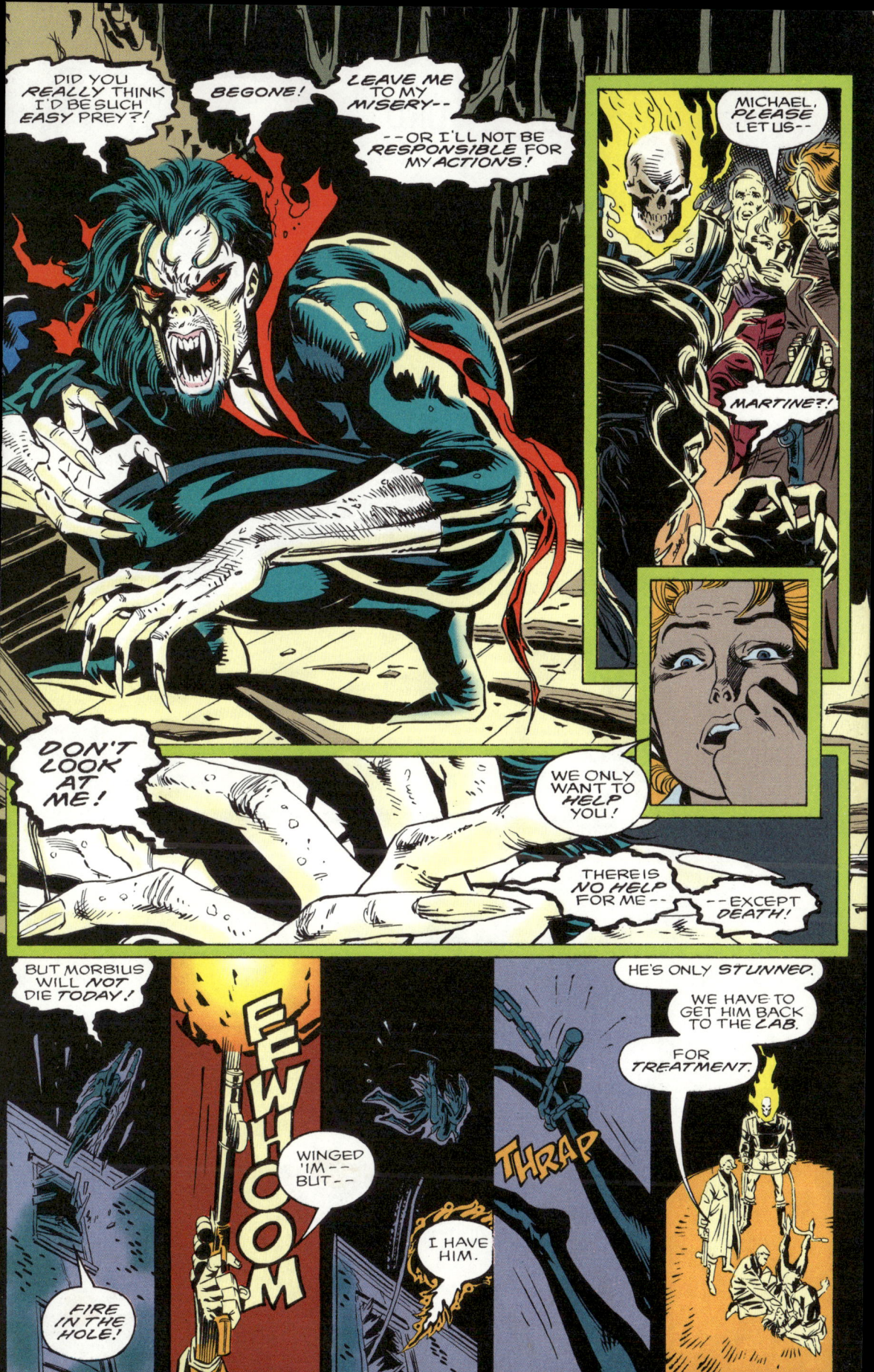

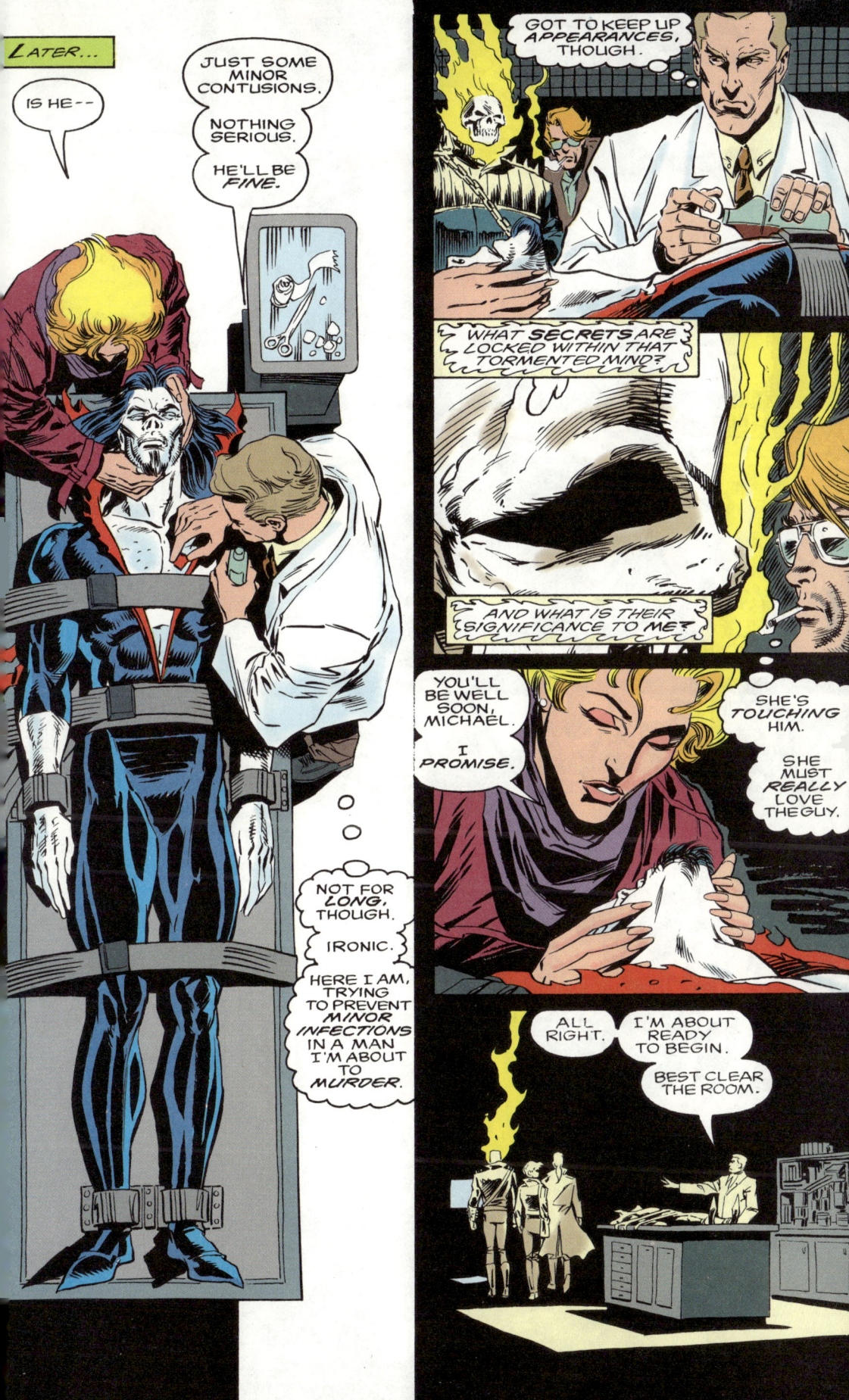

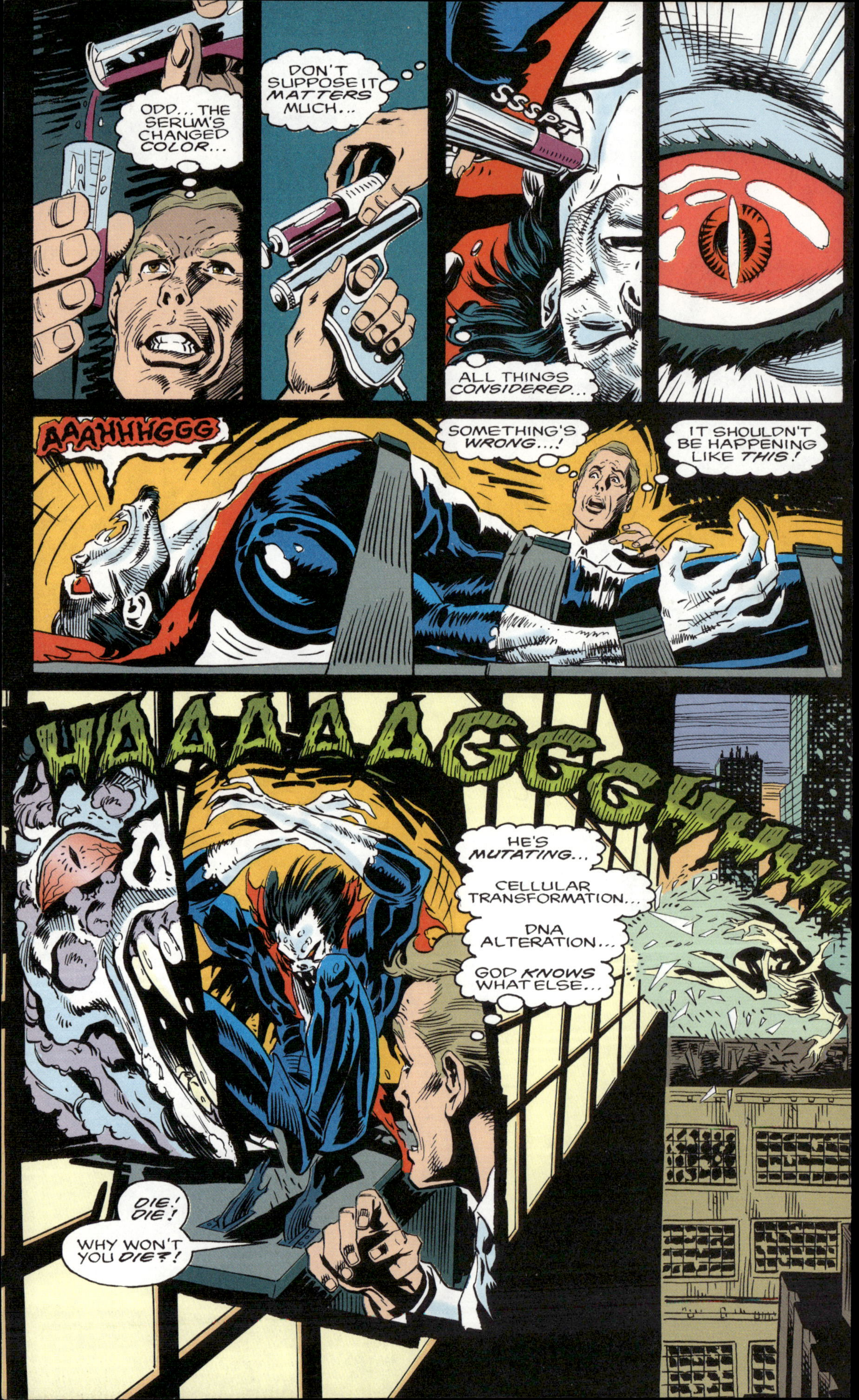

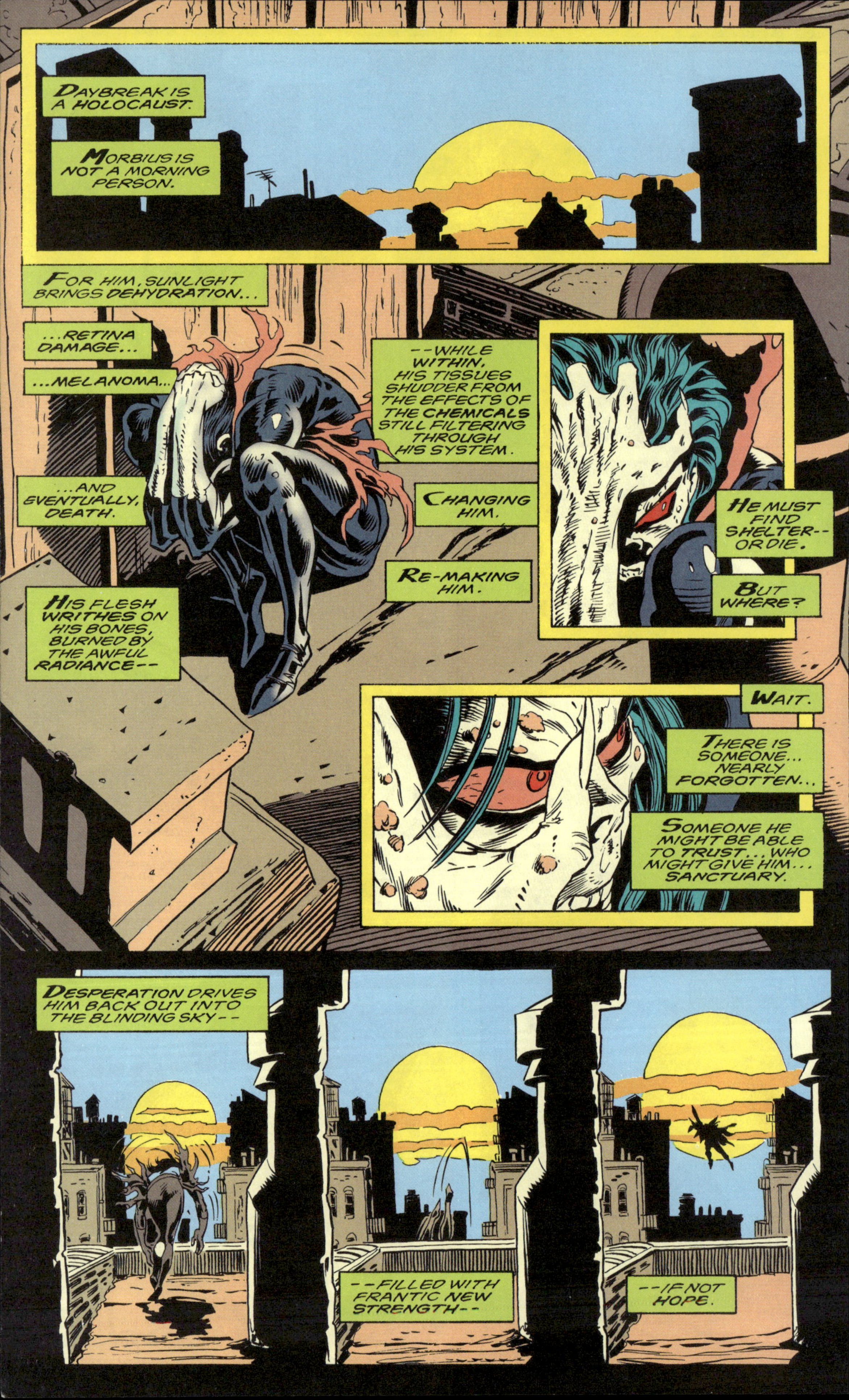

DAYBREAK IS A HOLOCAUST.

MORBIUS IS NOT A MORNING PERSON.

FOR HIM, SUNLIGHT BRINGS DEHYDRATION...

...RETINA DAMAGE...

...MELANOMA...

...AND EVENTUALLY, DEATH.

--WHILE WITHIN, HIS TISSUES SHUDDER FROM THE EFFECTS OF THE CHEMICALS STILL FILTERING THROUGH HIS SYSTEM.

CHANGING HIM.

RE-MAKING HIM.

HE MUST FIND SHELTER-- OR DIE.

BUT WHERE?

HIS FLESH WRITHES ON HIS BONES, BURNED BY THE AWFUL RADIANCE--

WAIT.

THERE IS SOMEONE... NEARLY FORGOTTEN...

SOMEONE HE MIGHT BE ABLE TO TRUST... WHO MIGHT GIVE HIM... SANCTUARY.

DESPERATION DRIVES HIM BACK OUT INTO THE BLINDING SKY--

--FILLED WITH FRANTIC NEW STRENGTH--

--IF NOT HOPE.

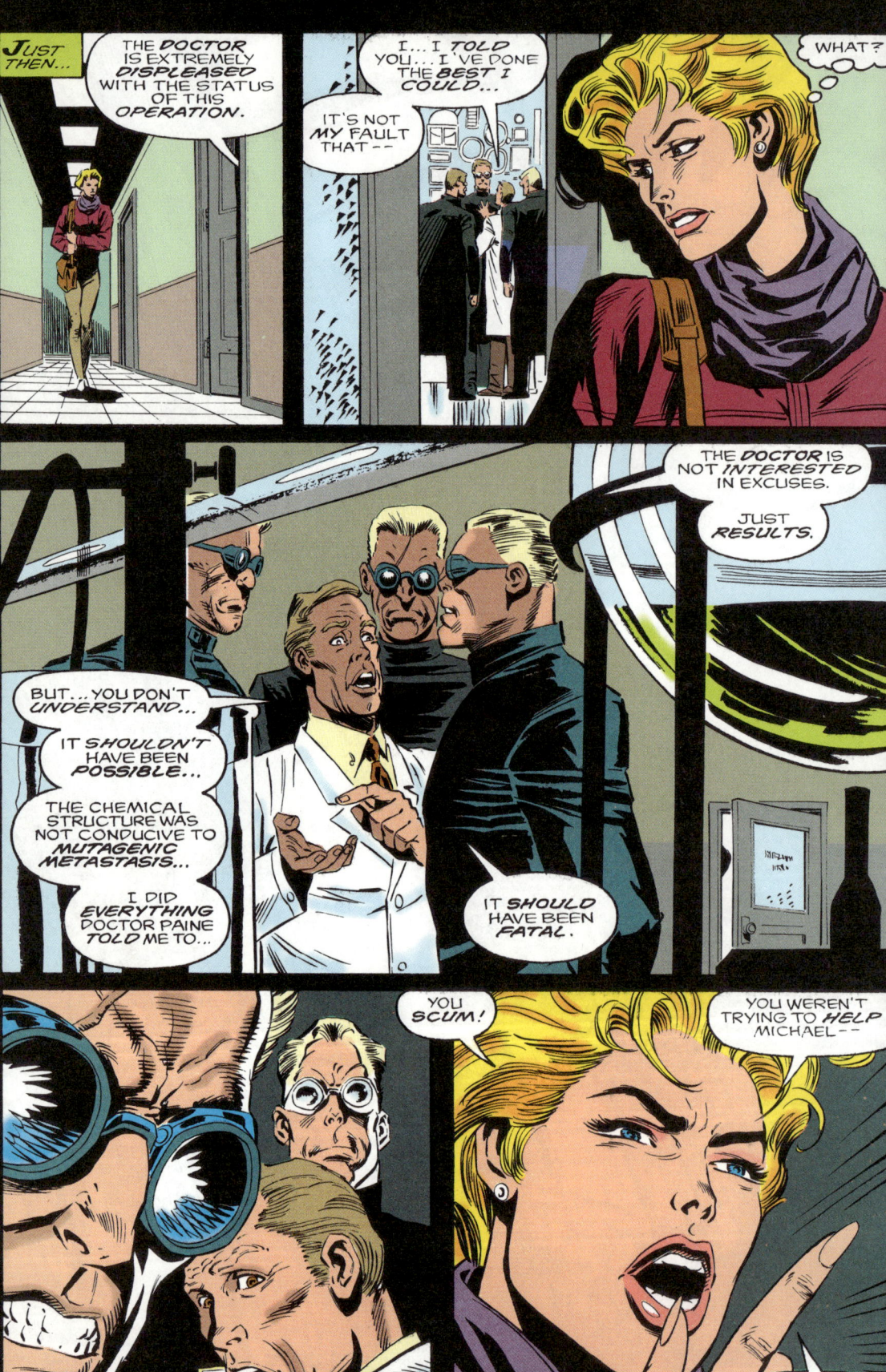

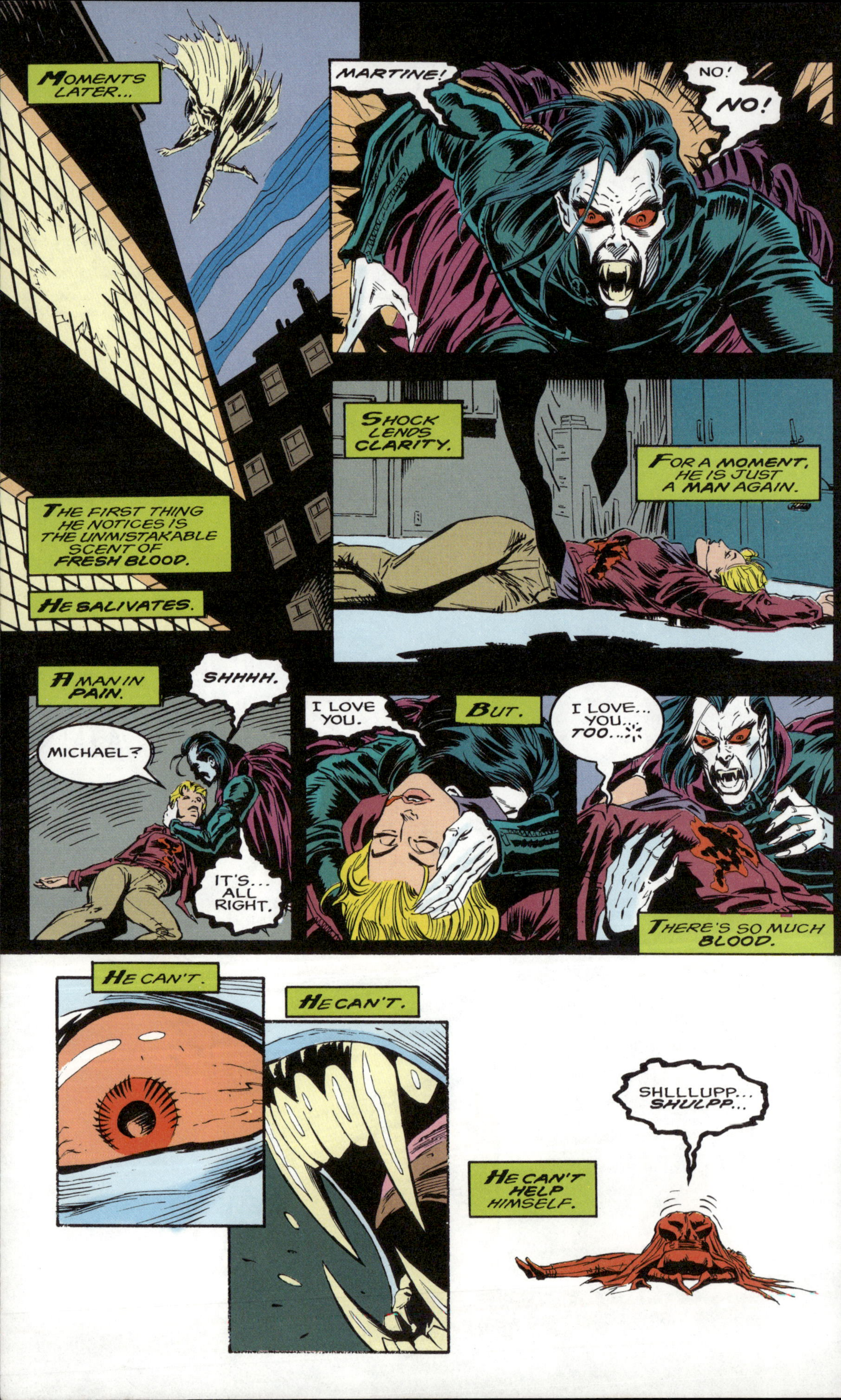

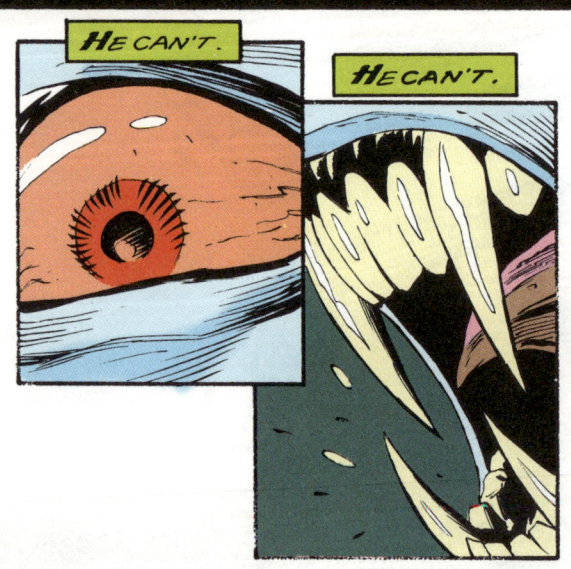

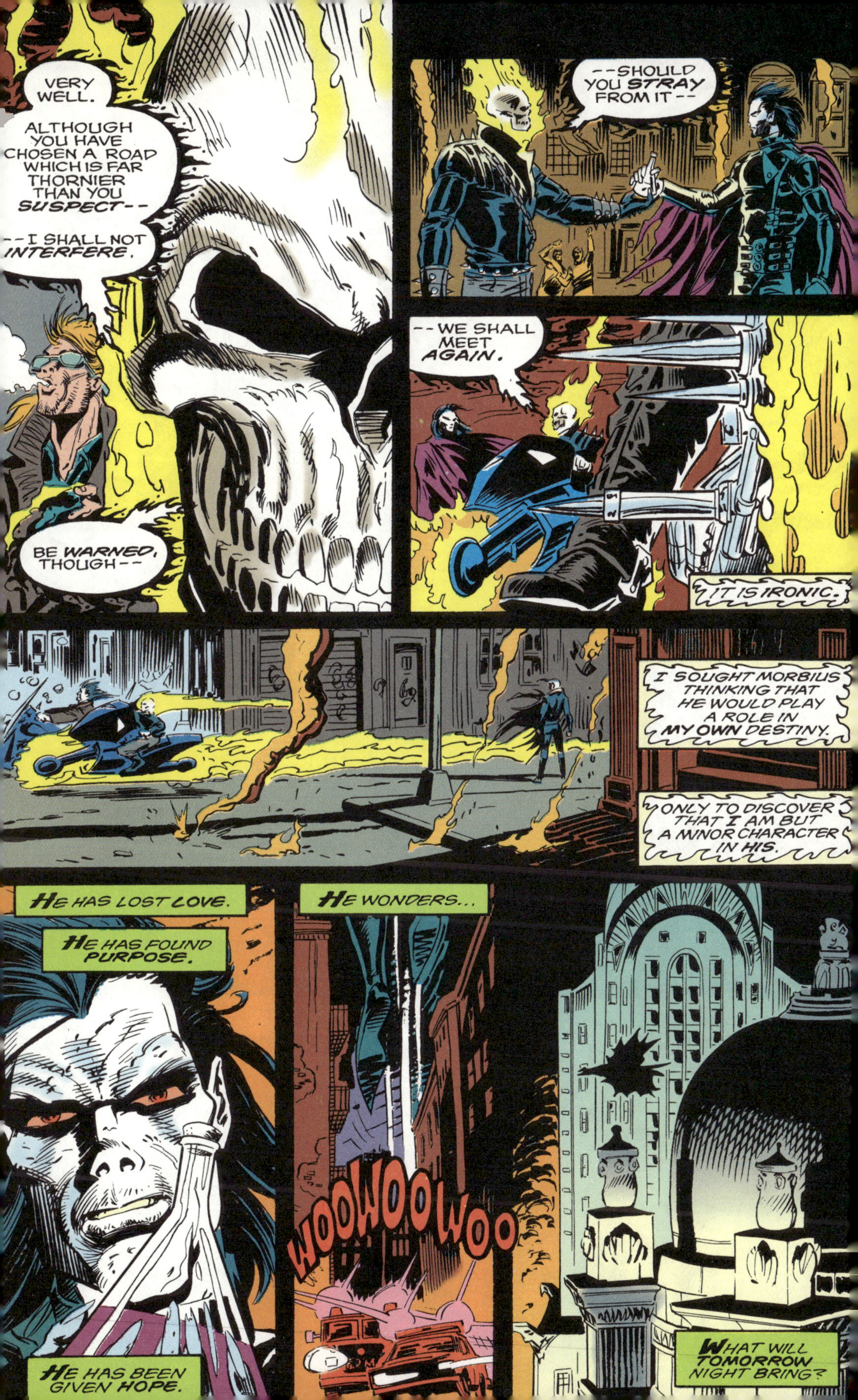

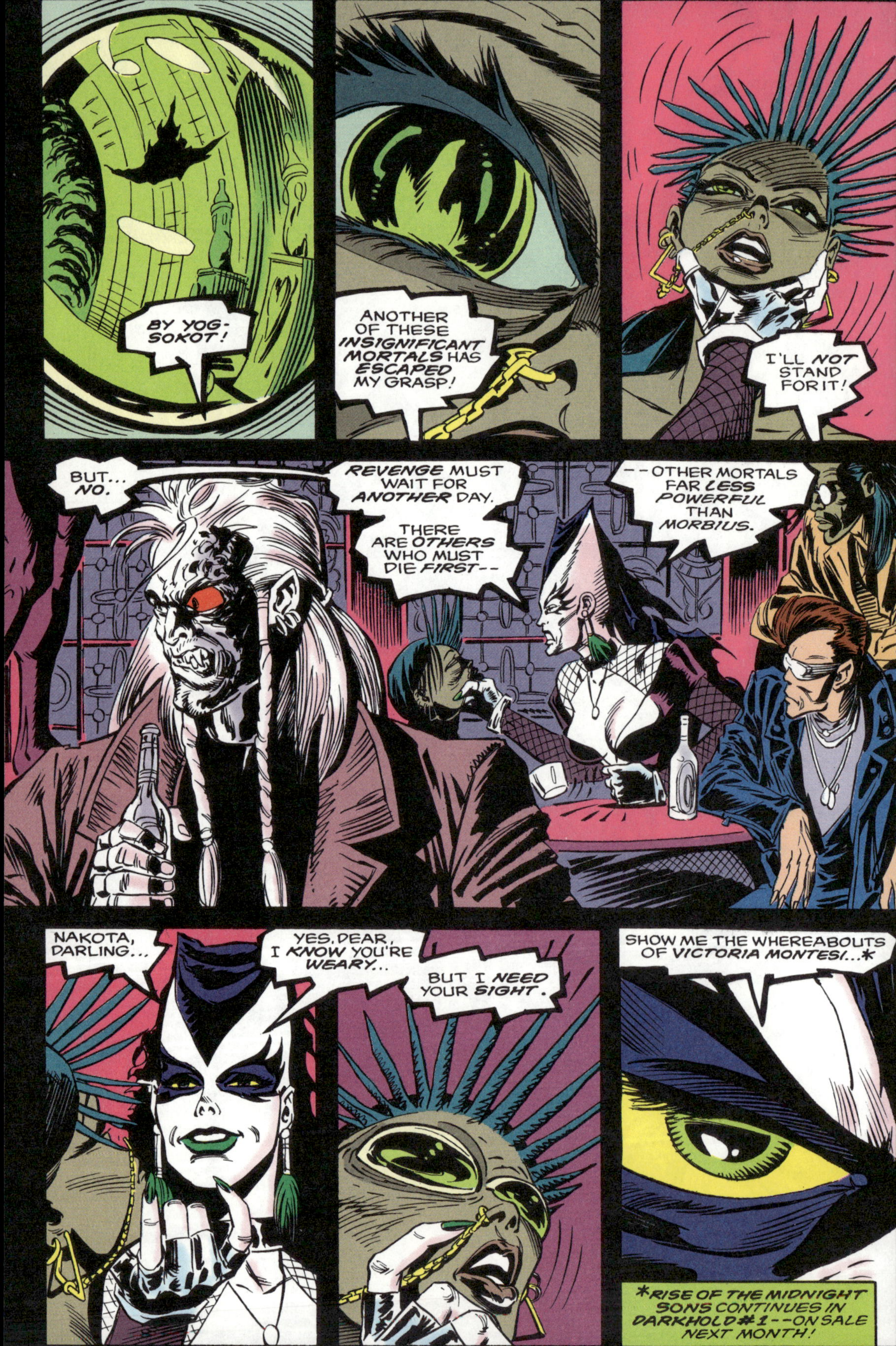

For eons, the walls between our earth and the supernatural realms have held fast ... until now. Now those walls are weakening, and LILITH, Queen of Evil, Mother of Demons, has risen from her slumber to shatter the walls and free her hellish spawn. Only the strangest of alliances can drive her back ... a union of old enemies and new heroes, in a battle forever to be remembered as the ...

DARKHOLD #1
PART 4

Writer: **CHRISTIAN COOPER**
Penciler: **RICHARD CASE**
Inker: **MARK McKENNA**
Colorist: **GLYNIS OLIVER**
Letterer: **PHIL FELIX**
Editor: **BOBBIE CHASE**
Managing Editor: **KELLY CORVESE**
Editor In Chief: **TOM DeFALCO**

GHOST RIDER #28   Part 1
SPIRITS OF VENGEANCE #1   Part 2
MORBIUS #1   Part 3
NIGHTSTALKERS #1   Part 5
GHOST RIDER #31   Part 6

BLACK LETTER

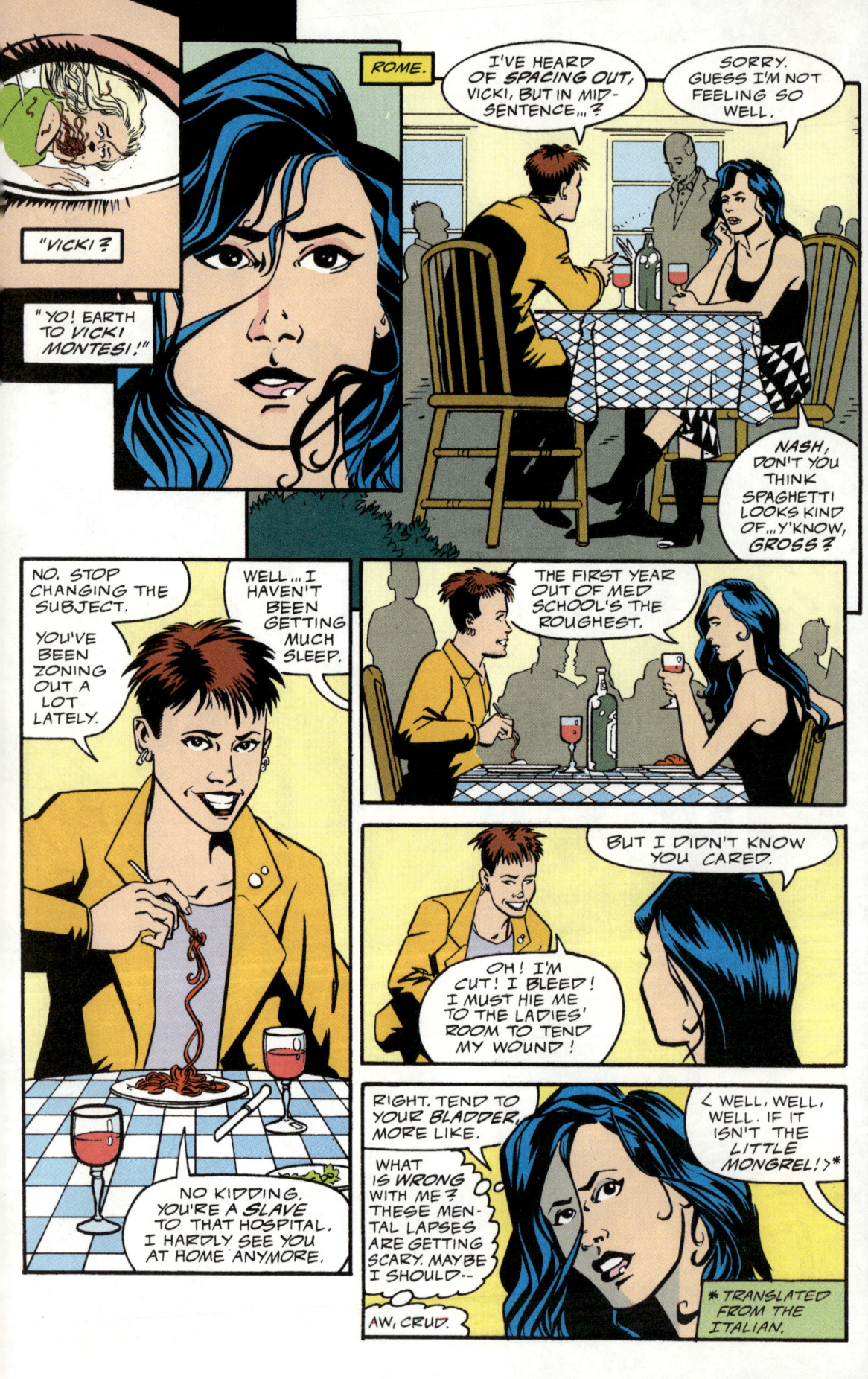

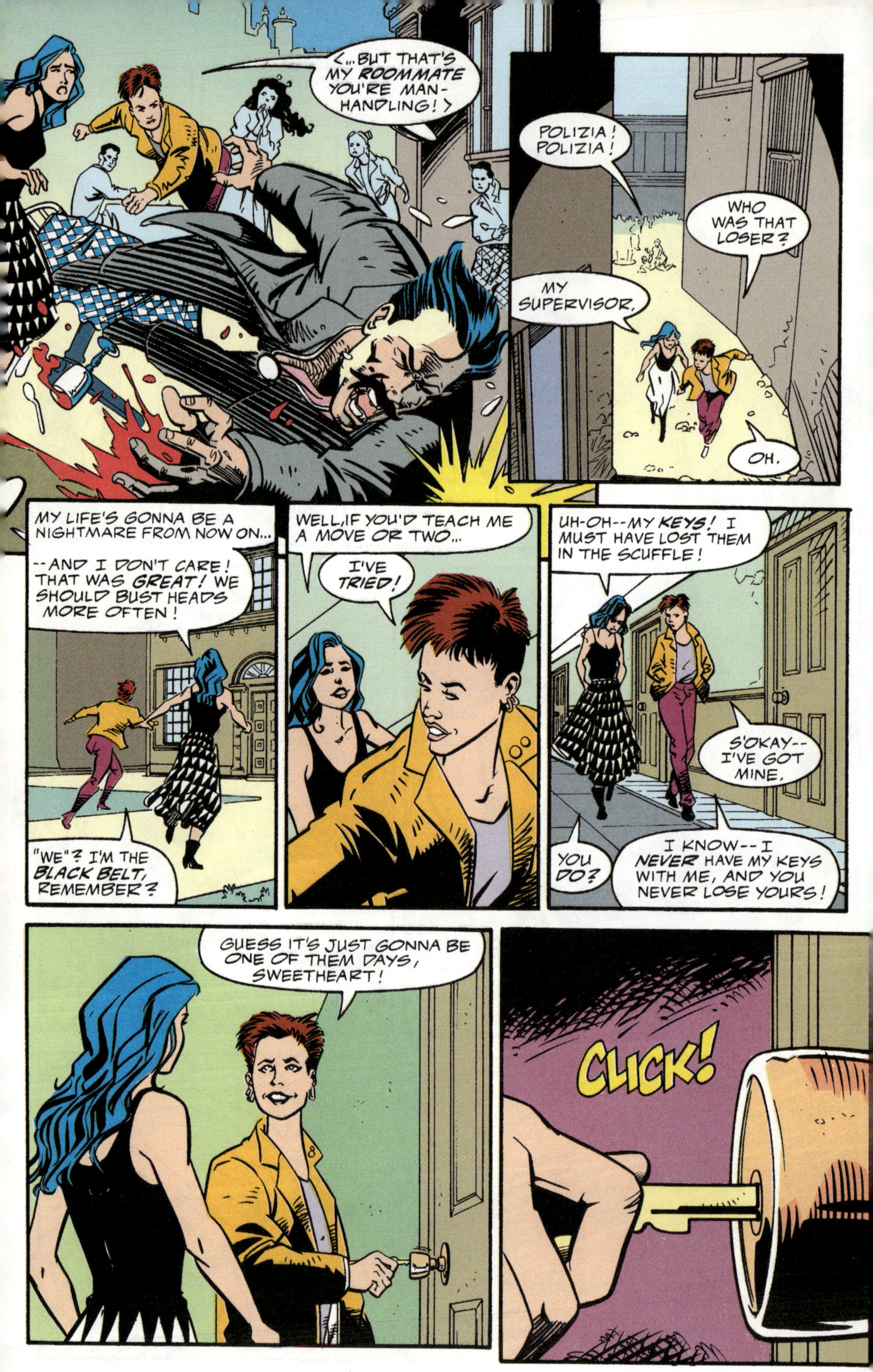

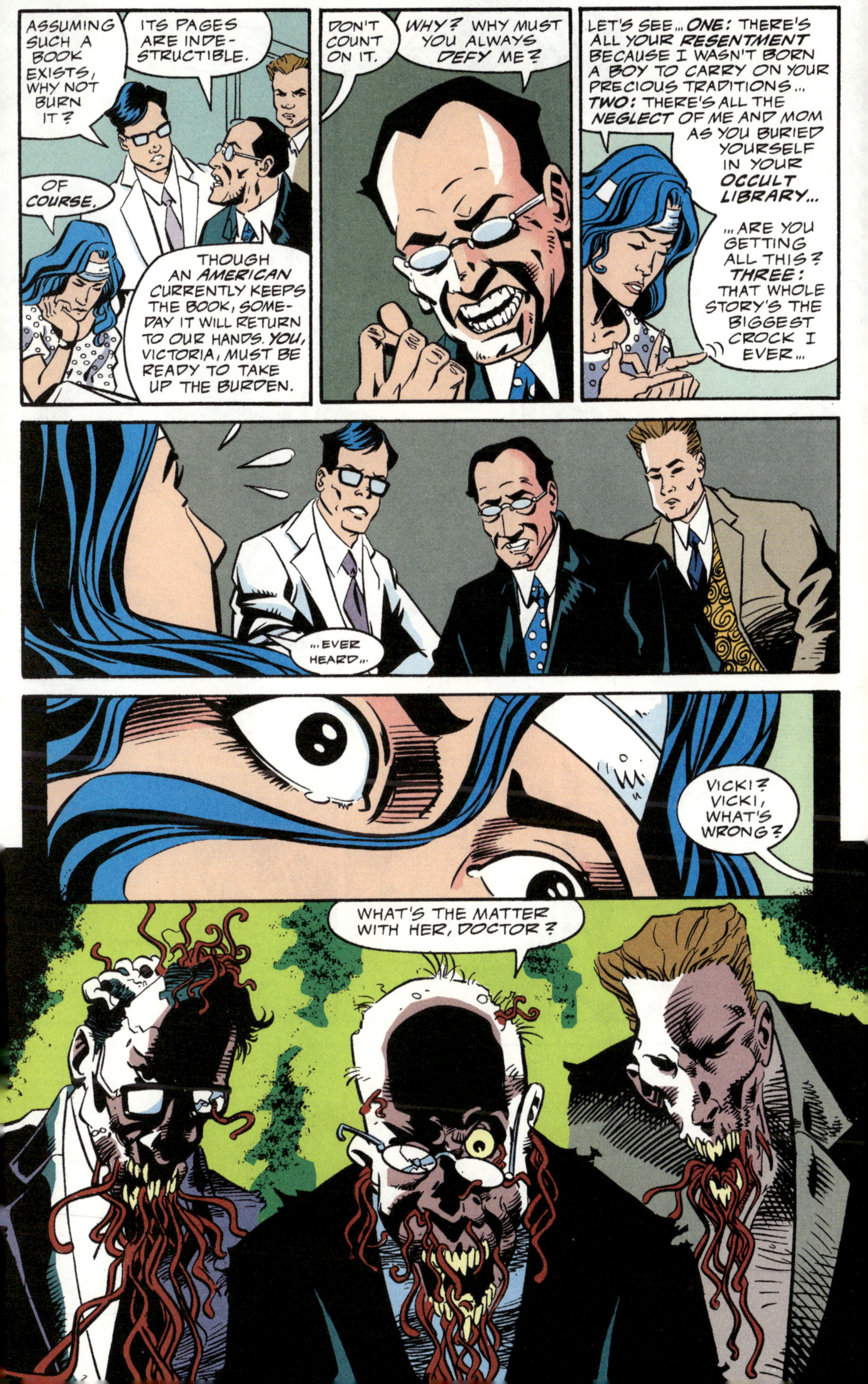

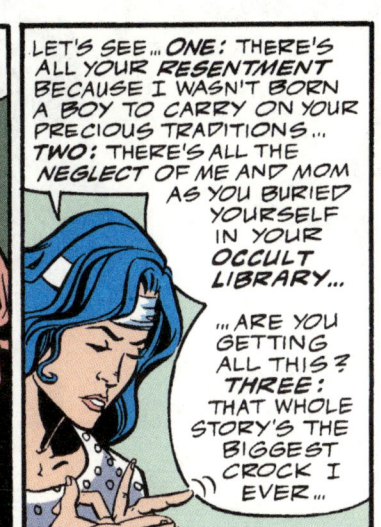

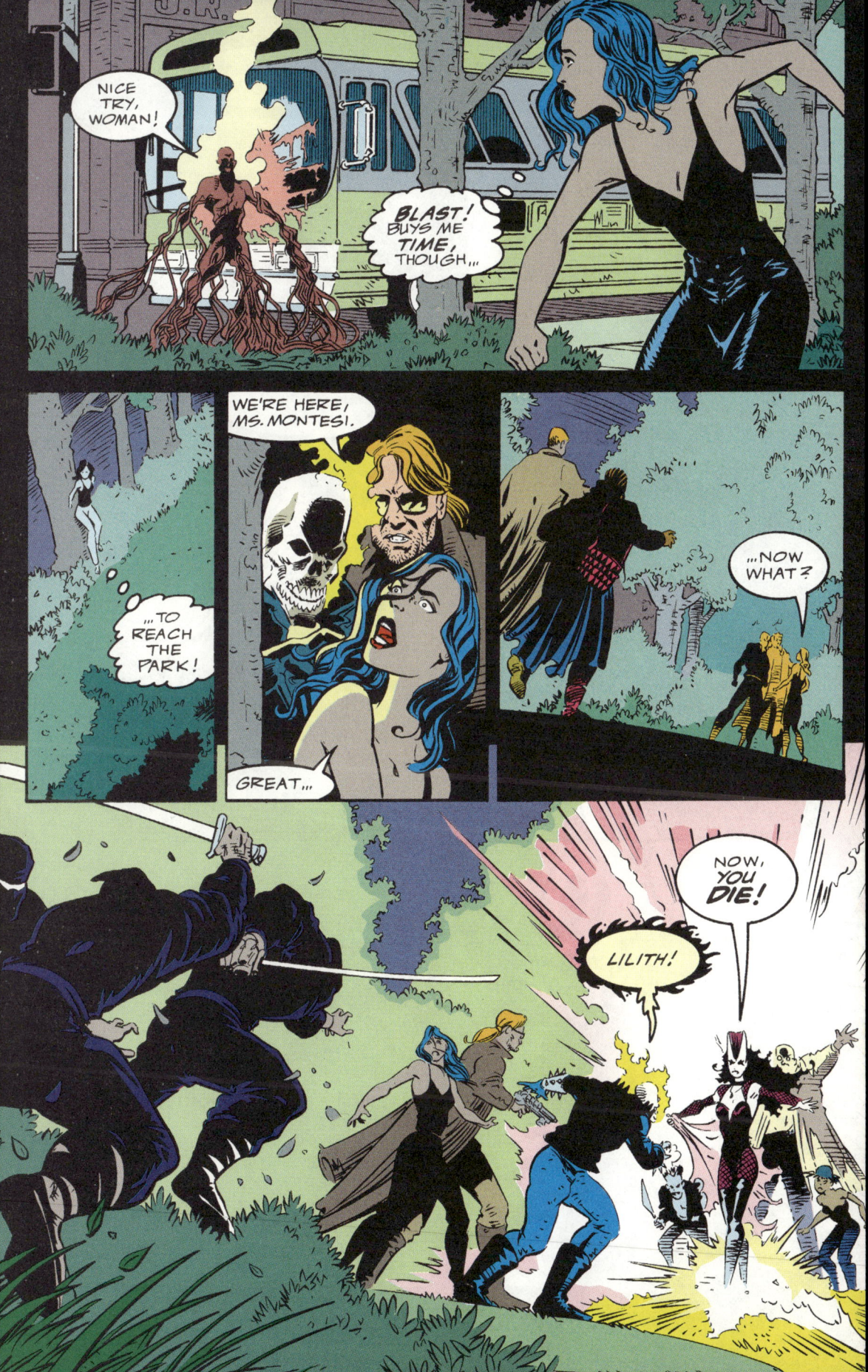

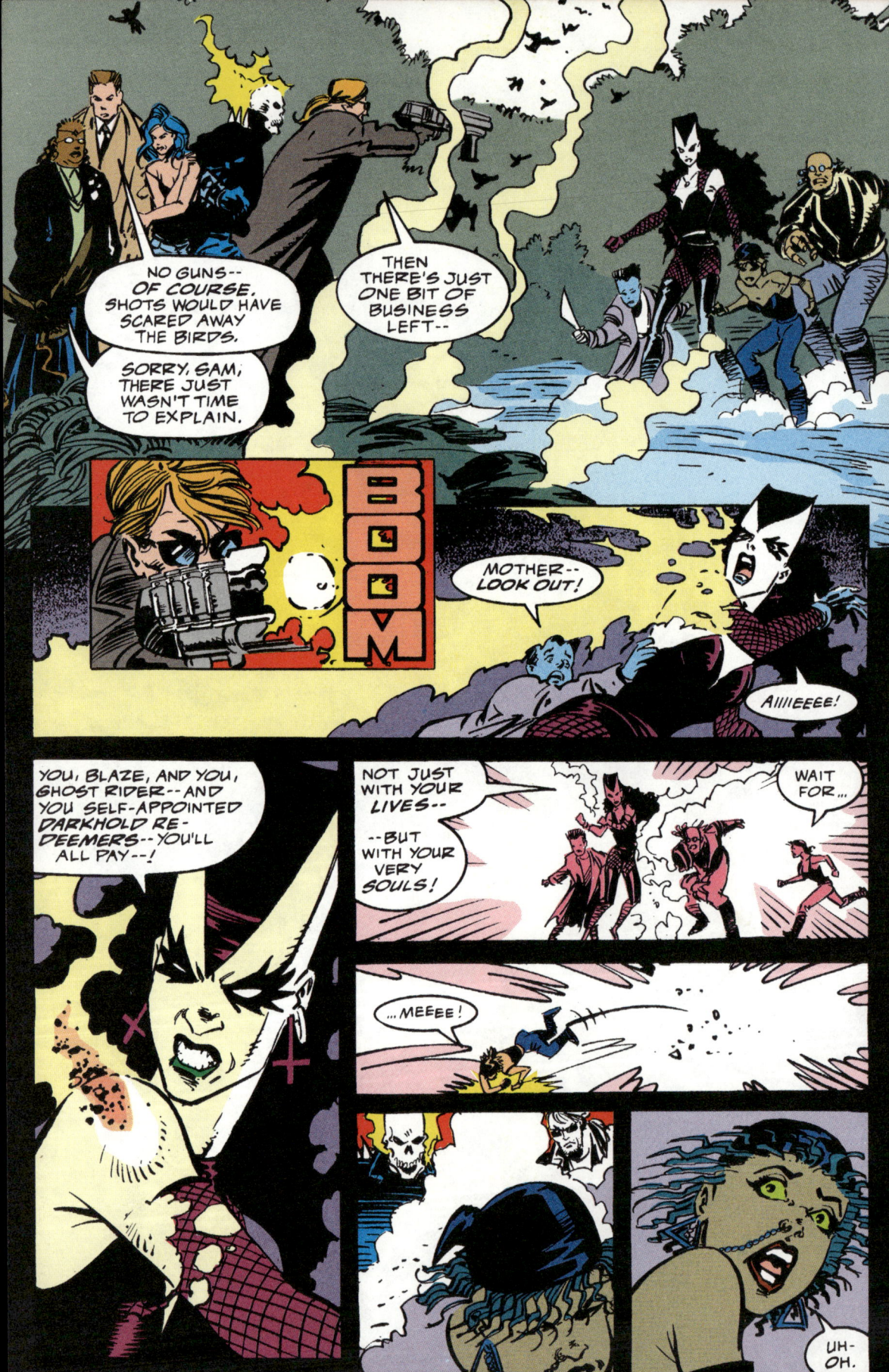

For eons, the walls between our earth and the supernatural realms have held fast ... until now. Now those walls are weakening, and LILITH, Queen of Evil, Mother of Demons, has risen from her slumber to shatter the walls and free her hellish spawn. Only the strangest of alliances can drive her back ... a union of old enemies and new heroes, in a battle forever to be remembered as the ...

NIGHTSTALKERS #1
PART 5

Writer: D.G. CHICHESTER
Penciler: RON GARNEY
Inker: TOM PALMER
Colorist: TOM PALMER
Letterer: JOHN COSTANZA
Editor: BOBBIE CHASE
Editor In Chief: TOM DeFALCO

GHOST RIDER #28   Part 1
SPIRITS OF VENGEANCE #1   Part 2
MORBIUS #1   Part 3
DARKHOLD #1   Part 4
GHOST RIDER #31   Part 6

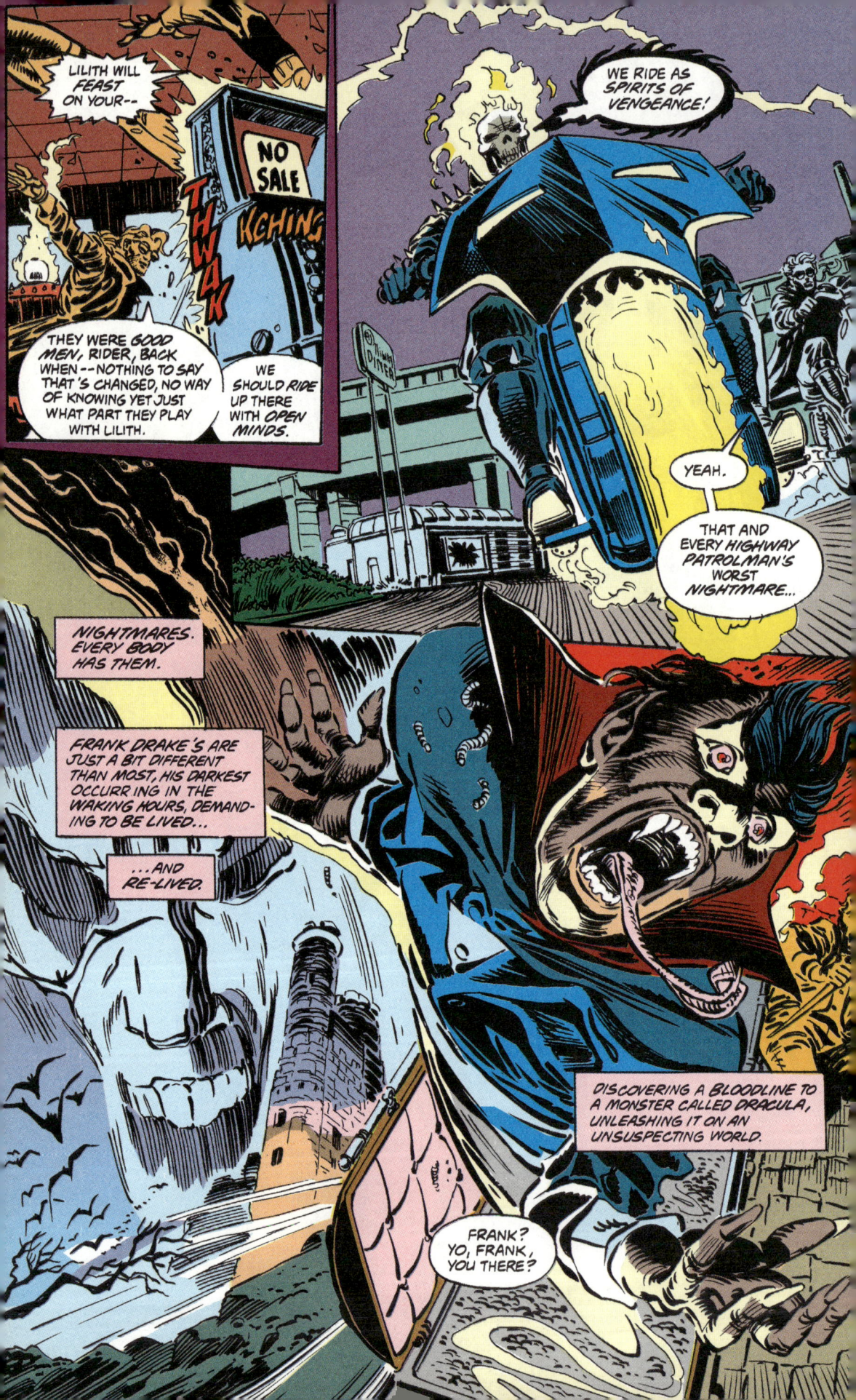

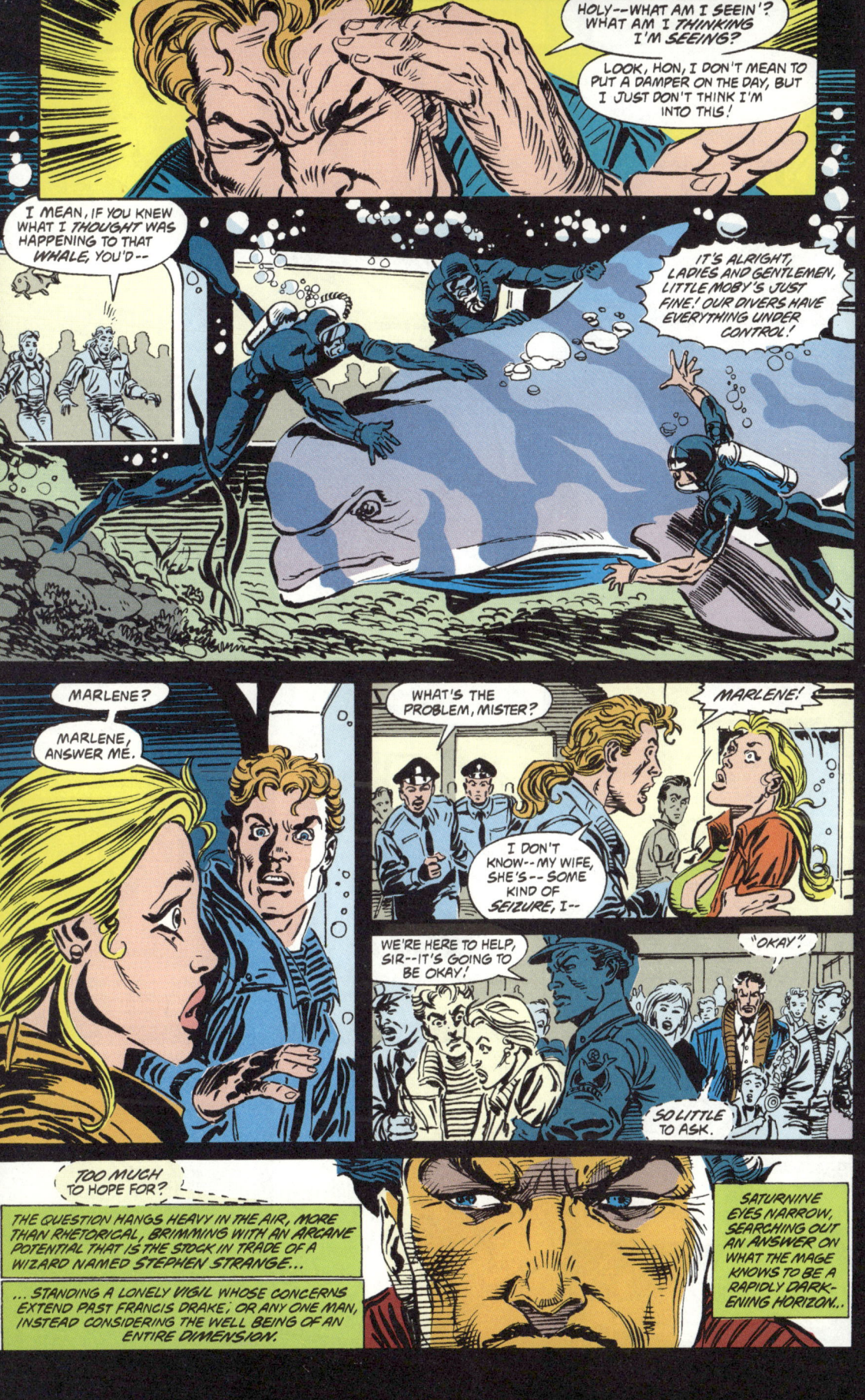

"IT WAS NEAR HALLOWEEN AND WE LET SOME OF THE PATIENTS--"

"IS ANYTHING TRULY INNOCENT, DIRECTOR RITEGRIG?"

"I TAKE IT BLADE WASN'T INTERESTED IN THE FESTIVITIES?"

"--IT WAS MEANT TO BE AN INNOCENT COSTUME PARTY."

"AND JUST WHAT DO YOU MEAN BY-- NEVER MIND, I DON'T WANT TO KNOW!"

"BLADE WAS NEVER INTERESTED IN MUCH OF ANYTHING, EXCEPT..."

"SOMETHING SEEMS TO HAVE CAUGHT HIS EYE, DIRECTOR."

"YES, CANDY CORN FANGS AND A PAPER TABLECLOTH CAPE."

"THAT'S ALL IT TOOK TO WIPE OUT ANY PROGRESS IN HIS TREATMENT AND TRIGGER HIS PHOBIA!"

"IMPRESSIVE...IF IT WASN'T SO ANTI-SOCIAL."

"A DOZEN ORDERLIES WERE NEEDED TO KEEP HIM FROM DRIVING A WOODEN STAKE THROUGH THAT BOY'S HEART."

"BLADE PUT SEVEN OF THEM IN THE HOSPITAL. TWO NEVER CAME BACK OUT..."

"I'M FAST FORWARDING TO ANOTHER SECTION..."

"...WE TRIED DIFFERENT THERAPIES, OF COURSE, BUT NONE HAVE BROKEN HIM OF THE CENTRAL DELUSION--"

"-- THAT HIS MOTHER WAS KILLED IN CHILDBIRTH BY A VAMPIRE NAMED "DEACON FROST" AND THAT BLADE HIMSELF WAS TAINTED BY ITS BITE!"

"PRECISELY THE REASON FOR A NEW TREATMENT, DIRECTOR RITEGRIG!"

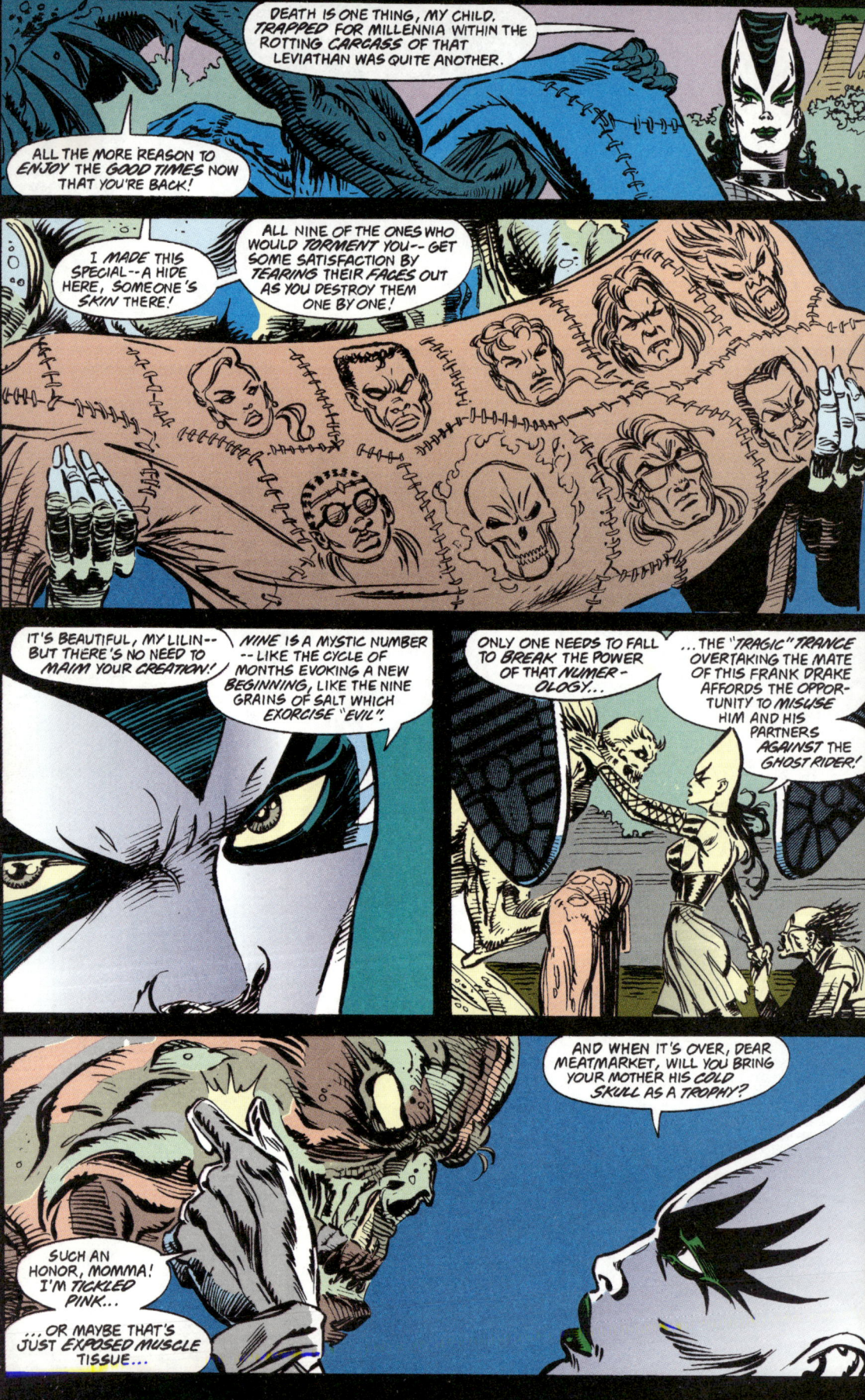

LONG TIME, HANNIBAL...

...BUT OLD HABITS *DIE HARD*, HUH?

KLICK

"SCREW RUSTY OLD KEYS," FRANKY...

THWIP THWIP THWIP

...I BROKE IN!

SOMEHOW I EXPECTED NO LESS, BLADE.

A *REUNION*, S'THAT IT? LET'S REALLY MAKE IT LIKE OLD TIMES-- WHEN YOU GUYS LEAVIN' AGAIN?

DON'T GIVE ME *GRIEF* ABOUT WHAT WAS, HANNIBAL-- I'VE GOT ENOUGH NOW WITH WHAT *IS*! MY WIFE'S-- IT'S SOME KIND OF *COMA*-- HER DOCTORS DON'T KNOW WHAT!

I NEED A... *SPECIALIST*. I NEED YOU TO HELP ME CONTACT *STRANGE*.

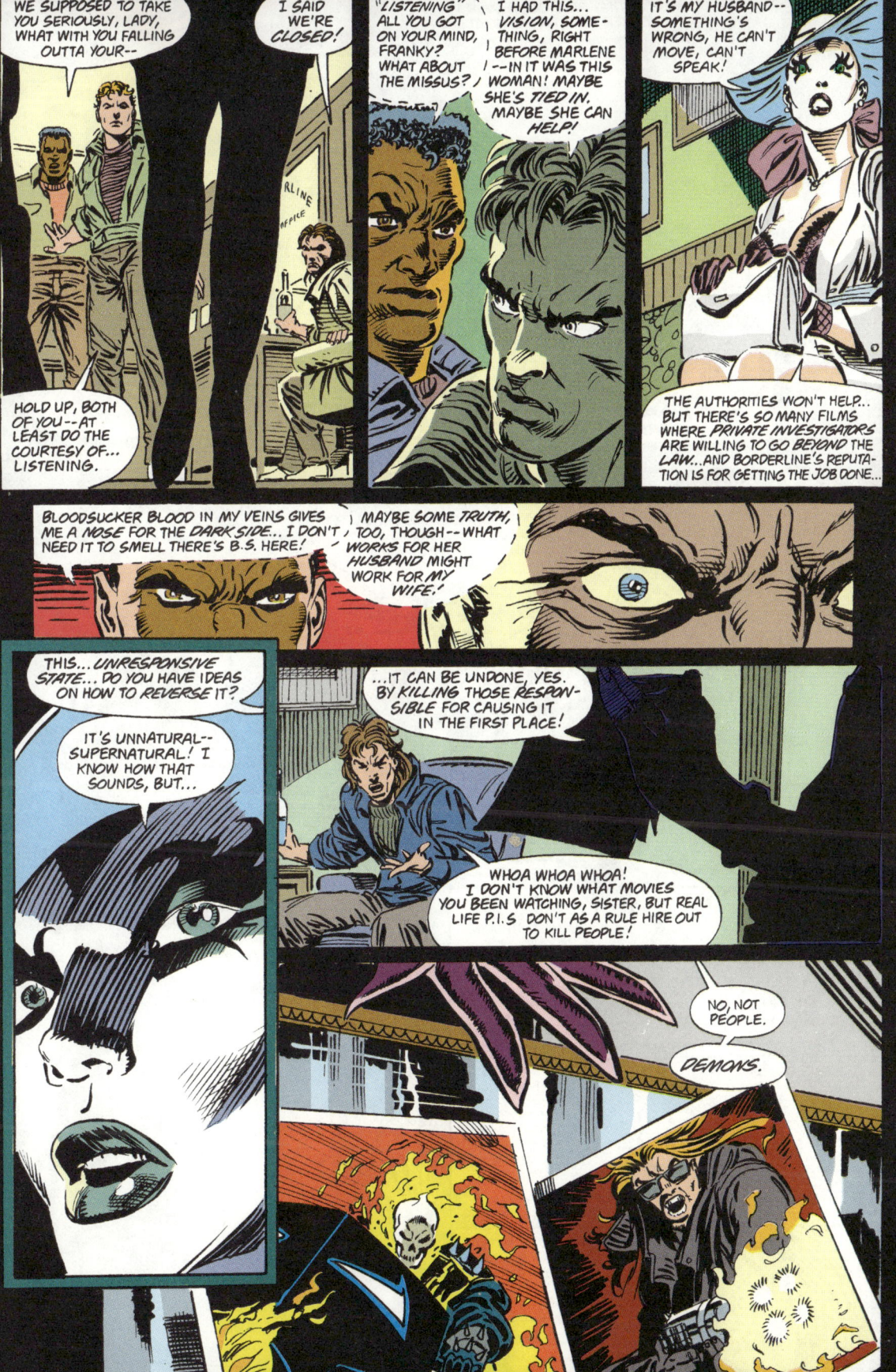

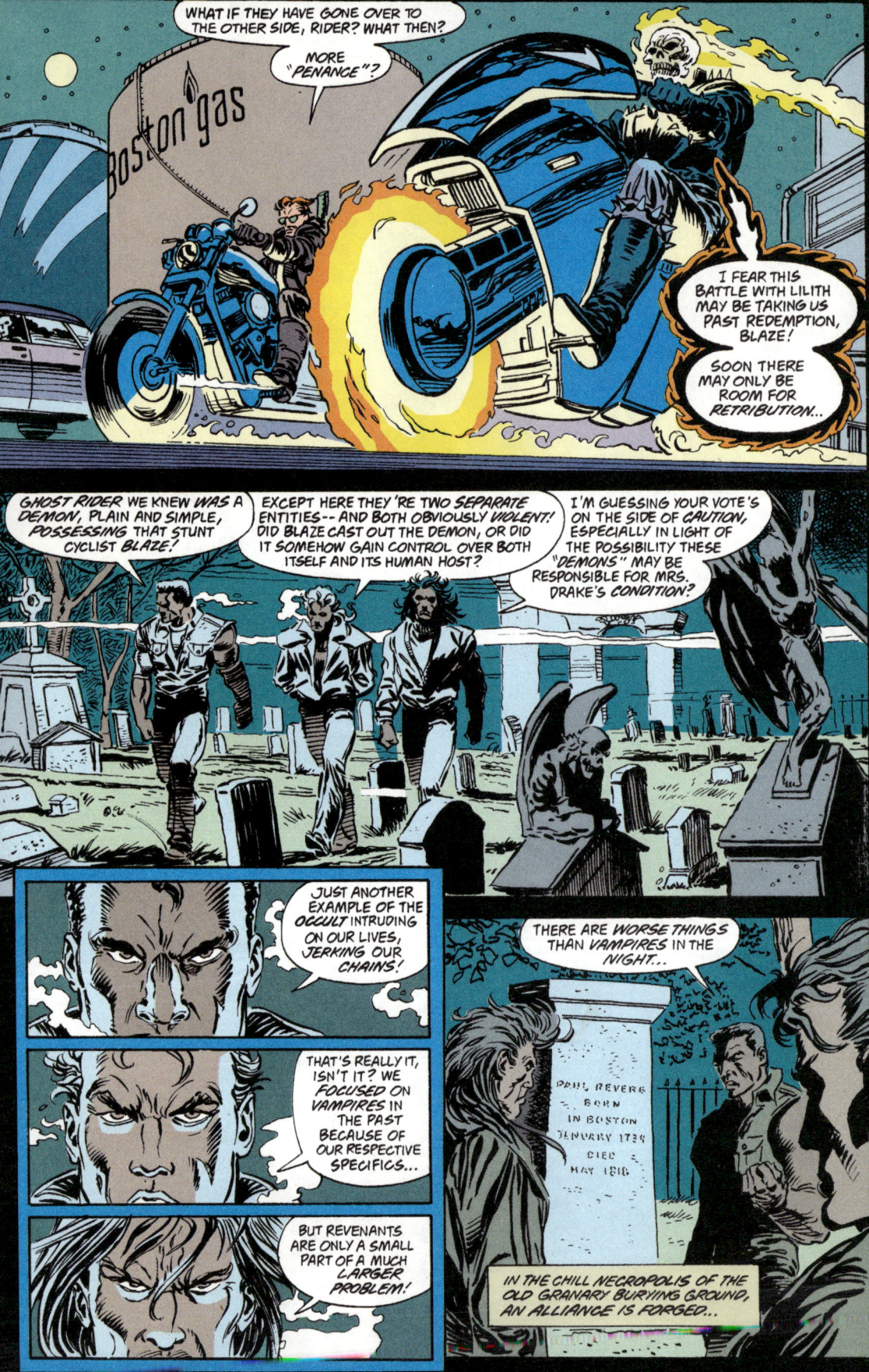

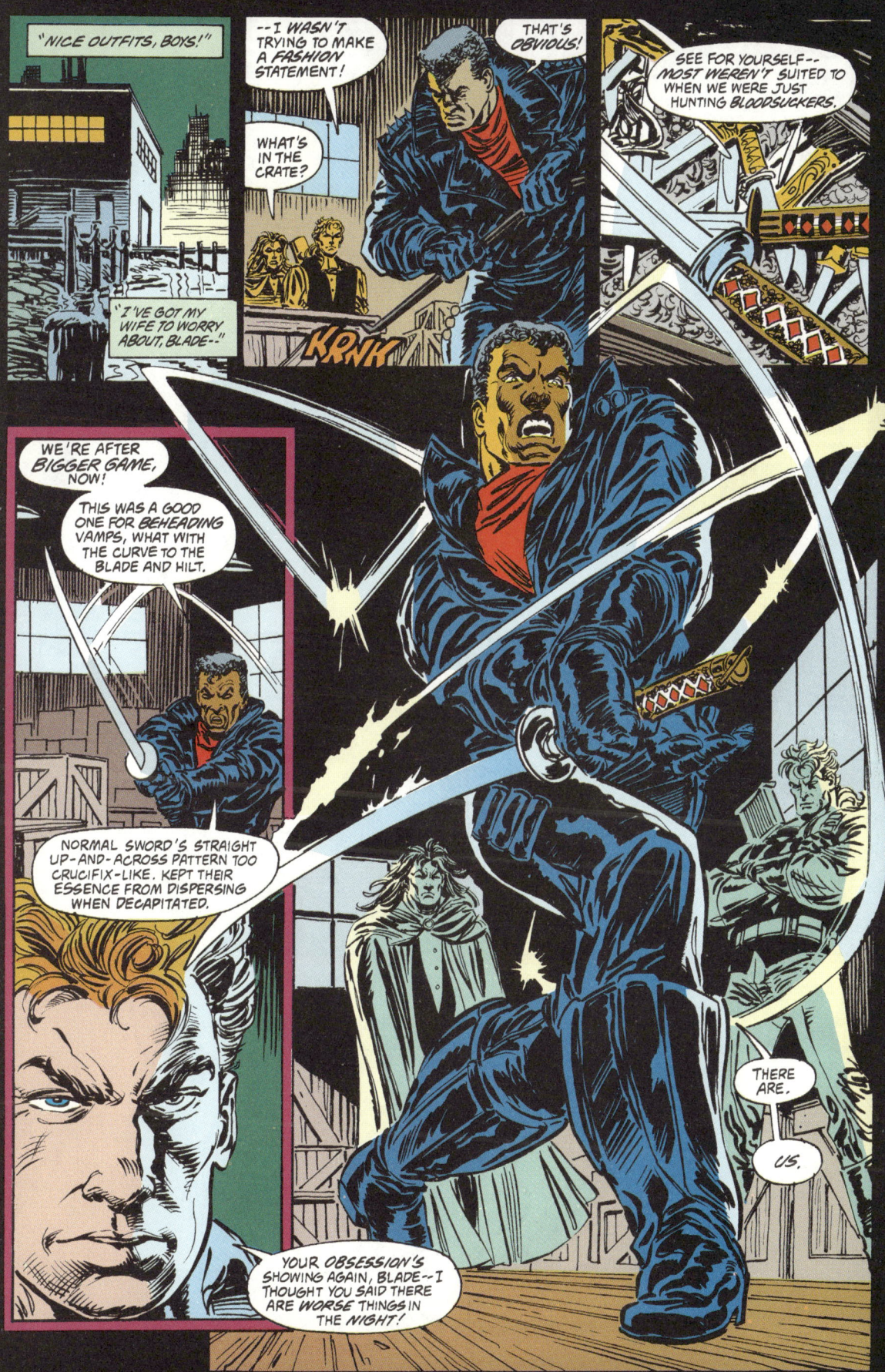

"WHAT HAPPENED TO THE AQUARIUM? WHAT AM I DOING IN A HOSPITAL?"

WHERE'S MY HUSBAND?

A NECESSARY MANIPULATION, MARLENE MCKENNA-DRAKE'S CATALEPSY PASSES AS QUICKLY AS IT CAME ON--

ARE YOU MY DOCTOR? ANSWER ME, PLEASE! ANSWER--

--BOTH CONDITIONS A RESULT OF ONE SMILING MAN'S MAGICS, THE TURN OF HIS LIPS CARRYING MORE CUNNING THAN WARMTH.

CAN'T HURT.

NEITHER CAN STAYING IN TOUCH WITH EACH OTHER ON THESE THINGS!

ANYONE GOING TO *BACK OUT*, NOW'S THE TIME...

THINK THEY'LL TAKE THE *BAIT*?

IF THEY'RE WHAT SHE SAYS, THEY'LL BE AFTER HER--IF THEY'RE AFTER HER, THEY'LL HAVE TRACKED HER TO BORDERLINE.

BACKING OUT'S *NEVER* BEEN AN *OPTION*, FRANKY.

THEY HAVE EYES, BUT THEY CANNOT SEE ME-- THANKS TO YOU, MOMMA DEAREST!

AND FROM THERE TO HERE. ANYONE GOT ENOUGH *FAITH* TO THINK A *CHURCH* IS REALLY GOING TO GIVE US AN *EDGE*?

OCCULT'S HAD US BY THE *SHORT HAIRS* SINCE DAY ONE-- ONLY THING NOW IS TO SEE IT DON'T GET HOLD OF NO ONE ELSE!

THIS IS GONNA BE GOOD...

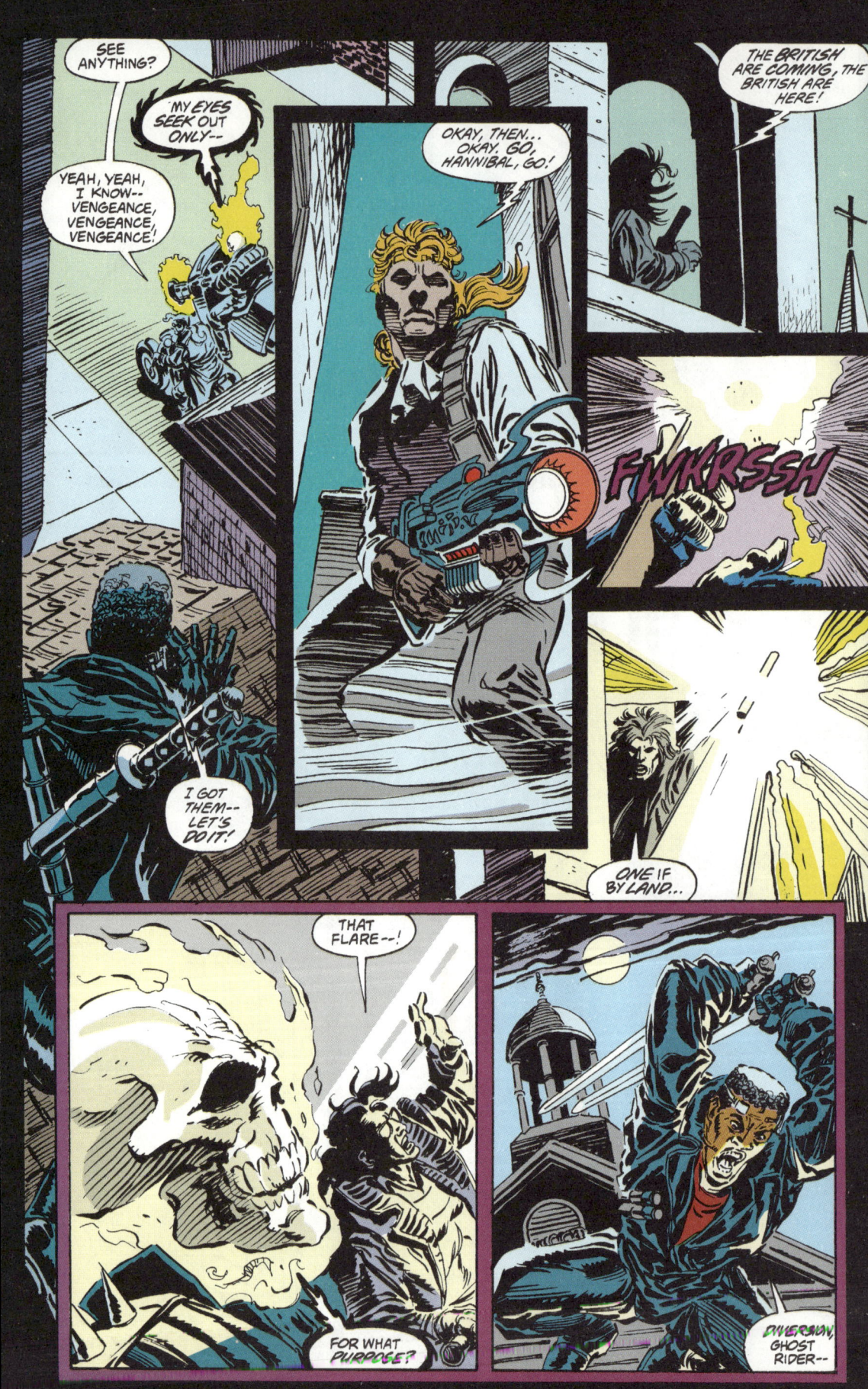

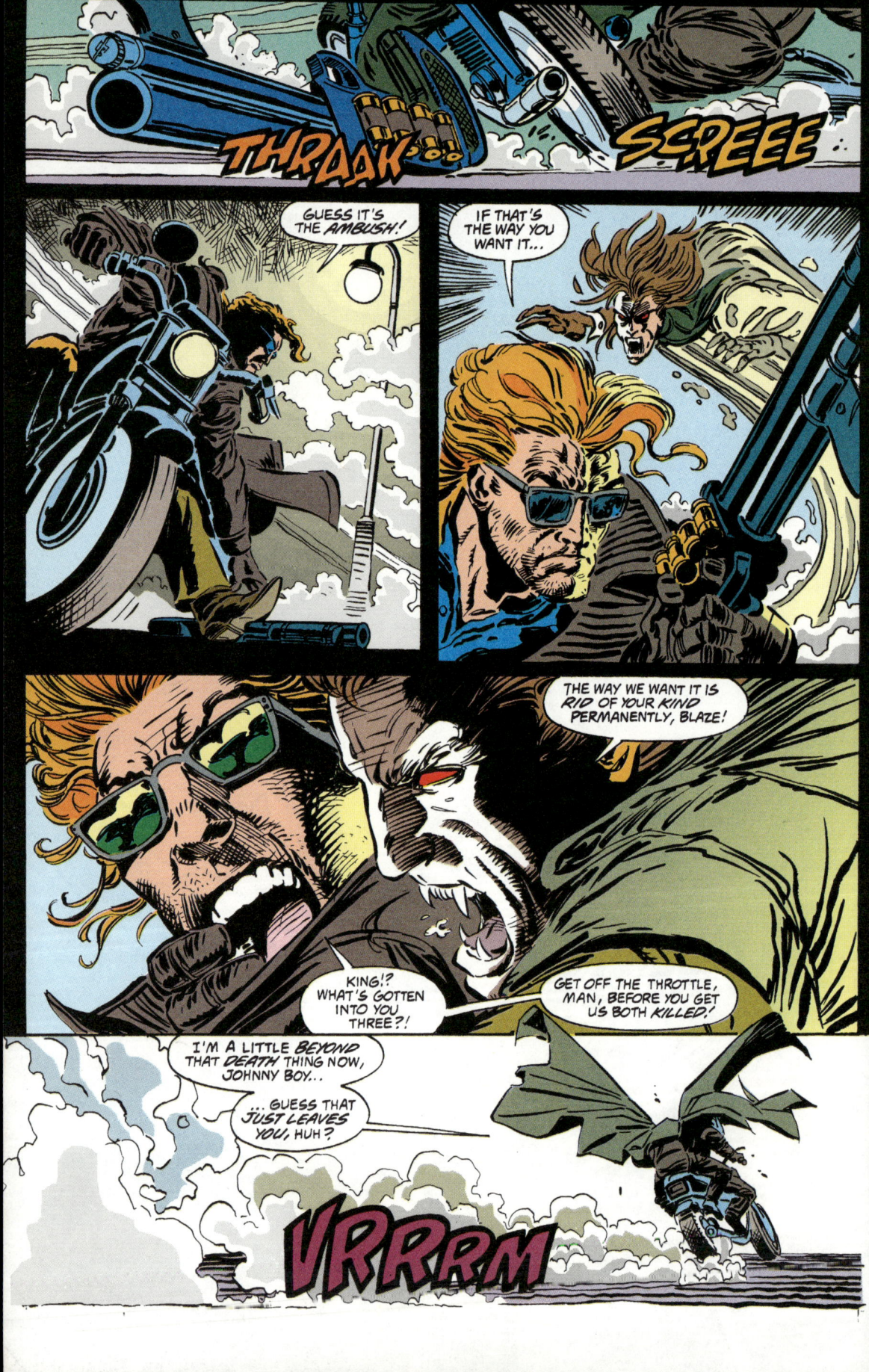

BREAK-- BREAK THE CURSE, OR WHATEVER... FOR THE CLIENT AND MARLENE!

KILL THEM, YES, EVEN ONE WILL BREAK THE NINE! THEN THE WAY IS CLEAR FOR MOMMA TO MAKE HER MARK!

THERE'S THAT SAME STENCH OF THE OCCULT AS THE LOCKER HAD IN THE OFFICE--

--BUT IT AIN'T COMING OFF THE BOOKENDS HERE!

IT SHOULD, THOUGH, IF THEY'RE THE CAUSE!

"IF."

THERE, FRANKY, YOU AND LINDA--

--TURN SOME HEADS!

KRAKOOM

For eons, the walls between our earth and the supernatural realms have held fast ... until now. Now those walls are weakening, and LILITH, Queen of Evil, Mother of Demons, has risen from her slumber to shatter the walls and free her hellish spawn. Only the strangest of alliances can drive her back ... a union of old enemies and new heroes, in a battle forever to be remembered as the ...

GHOST RIDER #31
PART 6

Writer: HOWARD MACKIE
Penciler: ANDY KUBERT
Inker: JOE KUBERT
Colorist: GREGORY WRIGHT
Letterer: JANICE CHIANG
Editor: BOBBIE CHASE
Editor In Chief: TOM DeFALCO

GHOST RIDER #28   Part 1
SPIRITS OF VENGEANCE #1   Part 2
MORBIUS #1   Part 3
DARKHOLD #1   Part 4
NIGHTSTALKERS #1   Part 5